Where
THE
Watermelons
GROW

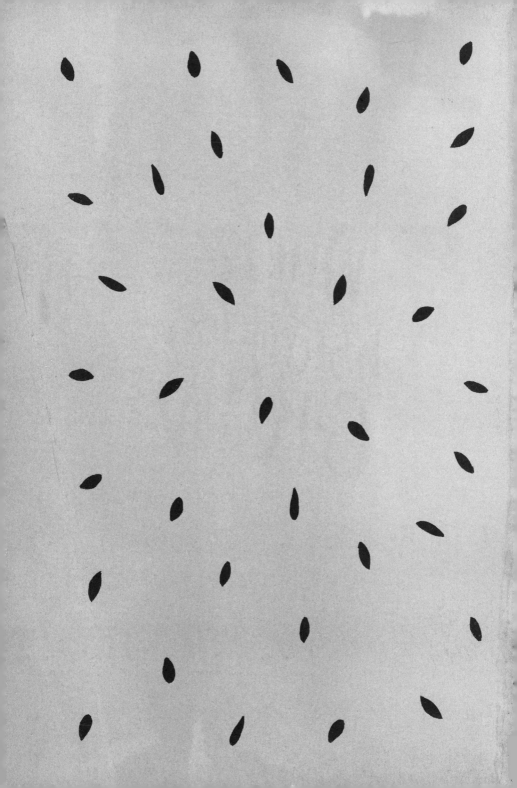

Where THE Watermelons GROW

a novel by
CINDY BALDWIN

HARPER
An Imprint of HarperCollinsPublishers

Library of Congress Cataloging-in-Publication Data

Names: Baldwin, Cindy, author.

Title: Where the watermelons grow / Cindy Baldwin.

Description: First edition. | New York, NY : Harper, an imprint of HarperCollins Publishers, [2018] | Summary: Twelve-year-old Della Kelly of Maryville, North Carolina, tries to come to terms with her mother's mental illness while her father struggles to save the farm from a record-breaking drought.

Identifiers: LCCN 2017034537 | ISBN 9780062665867 (hardcover)

Subjects: | CYAC: Schizophrenia—Fiction. | Mental illness—Fiction. | Farm life—North Carolina—Fiction. | Family problems—Fiction. | Droughts—Fiction. | North Carolina—Fiction.

Classification: LCC PZ7.1.B3568 Whe 2018 | DDC [Fic]—dc23 LC record available at https://lccn.loc.gov/2017034537

Typography by Erin Fitzsimmons

18 19 20 21 22 CG/LSCH 10 9 8 7 6 5 4 3

First Edition

For Shannon,

who believed in Della before I did,

and who held on to hope for this book when I couldn't

CHAPTER ONE

On summer nights, the moon reaches right in through my window and paints itself across the ceiling in swirls and gleams of silver.

I lay in bed, the sheet on top of me as hot and heavy as a down quilt, listening to the roar of the box fans that weren't doing a single thing to keep the heat out of my bedroom. I'd gone to bed hours earlier, but it was too hot to sleep—too hot to do anything but lie there watching the moonlight shift across the ceiling, thoughts spinning through my head like the wind on the bay right before a storm breaks. On the other side of the room, baby Mylie snored in her crib.

Only a baby could sleep on a night as hot as this.

I closed my eyes, letting a string of numbers appear against my darkened eyelids. Doubling numbers as far up as I could go: it was a trick Daddy had taught me, and my favorite way to fall asleep—a problem interesting enough to keep my mind focused, but not so hard that I couldn't drift off when I was ready. *One. Two. Four. Eight. Sixteen. Thirty-two. Sixty-four.*

I'd made it all the way to *One thousand twenty-four times two is two thousand forty-eight* when I finally gave up trying to concentrate my way into sleep and slid my legs over the side of the bed, the cool carpet hitting my toes a tiny little shot of relief in all that heat. The clock on my nightstand read 12:03. I tiptoed out of my bedroom and through the dark hallway so nobody could hear I was awake and come tell me off for it.

But I wasn't the only one awake.

Mama was sitting at the kitchen table, her pale skin strange and greenish in the light from the left-open fridge. A plate of watermelon slices sat on the table in front of her, and she was looking at them with the same look I have when I'm taking a test in English class. She used the tip of a knife to flick the black seeds out of each slice, one by one, not seeming to care that they were landing all over the table and the floor. One seed had stuck itself to her forehead, hanging there like a little bug just above her crunched-up concentrating eyebrow.

"Mama?" My voice was quiet and a little shaky in the silent kitchen, with only the refrigerator hum to back me up.

It was one of Daddy's sliced-up watermelons on that plate. My daddy grows the sweetest watermelons in all of North Carolina. He grows other things, too, like wheat and peanuts in his big fields and squash and berries in his small ones, but the watermelons are my favorite. Biting into one of those ruby-red slices is like tasting July, feeling that cold juice hitting your tongue like an explosion.

I like to take a spoon and dig out round bites so big they barely fit into my mouth, but Mama's always after me to slice them in neat little pyramids. "So that everyone can enjoy them," she says, glaring at the holes my spoon left, and every time she does I know she's thinking about all the germs that came from my lips touching that spoon touching the watermelon.

But whatever she was doing to those slices on that plate was way worse than obsessing over a few germs.

Watermelon is near about my favorite thing in the world to eat—if I'm hungry enough, I can eat almost a whole one by myself, which Daddy says is pretty impressive for a girl who's barely twelve and not yet five feet tall—but right then, the taste of all those remembered melons on my tongue was sour and awful.

I cleared my throat. "Mama?" I said again, louder this time.

"Della," she said. "You oughta be in bed."

"I just had to get a drink of water." I wiggled my toes against the bare linoleum floor. It was sticky where it hadn't gotten cleaned up enough after Mylie threw her sippy cup down there when she pitched a fit about going to bed.

Where sleeping was concerned, Mylie pitched a *lot* of fits.

"What are you doing, Mama? Don't you want to be in bed, too?"

"No."

I inched into the kitchen a little at a time, keeping my feet away from the seeds all over the floor and reaching for a clean glass from the cupboard. I ignored the open fridge with Mama's special no-germs-here water-filtering pitcher and filled my cup with tap water from the sink. I didn't want to know what Mama was doing. It felt like the long-ago bad time all over again, and I didn't want to know a single thing more about any of it. So all I said was, "Do you know you got a watermelon seed stuck above your eye?"

Mama's fingers flew to her forehead, picking the seed off and flicking it onto the tabletop real quick, like it might bite her. "I don't like these. There's just too many of them. I don't want you eating any, okay? And I don't want you feeding them to Mylie, either. I don't want them crawling around in your tummies and making you sick."

The glass of water froze in my hand halfway to my mouth. I looked at Mama and looked at her some more, wishing so hard that I hadn't gotten out of bed in the first place. Wishing I was asleep like I should have been, so that I wouldn't be here seeing Mama acting like this.

I drank up all my water and put the cup in the sink. Sometimes I liked to put my water cups on the counter, so I could keep drinking out of them and didn't have to wash them out between, but anytime I did that, Mama got on my case about all the germs my mouth had left on there. I never knew what she thought was going to happen—it wasn't like those mouth germs were going to crawl down the sides of the glass and onto the counter— but she sure didn't like for me to leave them.

"Listen," I said, taking a deep breath and pretending I was talking to Mylie instead of to Mama. More than anything I just wanted to go back into my bed and close my eyes and pretend I'd never come in here in the first place, but I knew I couldn't do that without it eating me up from the inside. Mama needed me. "I'm gonna close the fridge door now, okay? And then I'm gonna help you clean up the watermelon, and I think you should go to bed, otherwise you'll be tired at church tomorrow. And I know you don't like that."

What Mama really didn't like was when *I* was tired at church, but she didn't like being tired herself, either, because she said it turned her into a mean-green-mama-monster.

Sure enough, Mama frowned. "Why are you still up, Della?" she asked, like I hadn't just told her a minute ago. "You need to be in bed, honey."

I sighed. "I know. I'm going there right now. You gonna come to bed, too?"

Her eyes snapped back to that plate of watermelon, and her fingers started up again with the knife. The seeds made wet little taps on the table as they hit it, *tap-tap-tap-tap-tap*. "No!" she said, and I felt my shoulders jump a little, because she was so loud she was almost yelling. "I can't go to sleep tonight. I need to take care of this watermelon."

I heard a door open down the hallway, and Daddy came out, looking tired. His feet were bare and his hair was sticking up all over his head.

"Suzanne," he said, "what's the matter?" Then he saw

me. "Della, what are you doing out of bed? You know it's after midnight, right?"

I sighed again, a loud one this time so that Daddy could hear it. "I was just getting a drink." It was Mama I was mad at, but I couldn't stop that mad creeping across the kitchen toward Daddy anyway. "Is that not allowed in this house anymore?"

"Don't sass," said Daddy, but he didn't sound upset. He never sounded upset. That's one of those things about my daddy—he's so calm and quiet that you can hardly hear him talk sometimes. "Did you get your drink?"

"Yeah. Good night."

I didn't look at Mama again, but I could still hear those watermelon seeds tap-tap-tapping on the table as I walked down the hallway.

"Suzanne, please come to bed now," Daddy said as I opened my bedroom door.

"Can't. Can't go to sleep. Too busy."

There was silence behind me. I pictured Daddy pushing his callused white fingers through his brown hair like he does when he's upset and can't figure out what to do about it. "Suzie," he said, and his voice was so quiet I could hardly hear it, "you need your sleep, sweetie. You know you need your sleep or you're gonna get sicker."

Mama didn't say anything. I pulled my bedroom door closed behind me carefully and slowly, leaving it open a crack by my ear, so I could still hear them.

"Suzanne. Come with me now, all right? Come on to bed, please."

"No!"

I swallowed. Mama was almost-yelling at Daddy just like she'd been almost-yelling at me. I peeked through the crack I'd made in my doorway and could just barely see him, there behind Mama with his hands on her elbows, trying to pull her up out of that chair.

"Suzie, sweetie, put that knife away."

"No!" Mama shouted again, louder this time. From the other side of the bedroom, Mylie started whimpering and shaking the bars of her crib.

"Leave me alone," Mama said. "Just leave me alone. I have to do this. It's important. I gotta keep the girls safe."

I tiptoed over and reached through the crib bars to put my hand on Mylie's head, feeling her soft strawberry-blond curls all wet from sleep sweating. She was sitting up, her fat fingers in fists around the bars.

"Shh," I whispered, and she quieted down. "It's all right, baby. Go back to sleep. You want I should tell you a Bee Story?"

"Stowy," Mylie repeated, wiggling her little body till she was lying back down on the mattress.

"All right," I said, sinking down on to my knees by

the crib, my voice still quiet and low. I reached my hand in through the crib bars and rubbed her back as I spoke. I could feel her start to settle, relaxing into the mattress, like my hand on her back was all she needed to feel safe. *Lucky baby.* "Way back a long time ago, when Grandpa Kelly was still a little boy and the farm belonged to *his* daddy, he was playing on the tractor when he fell off and got a big old cut right down his leg. It was long and deep, and his parents knew if they took him to a doctor it would need stitching and medicine and might never heal good enough for him to walk normal. So they didn't take him to a doctor. They took him to the Quigleys."

I leaned my face against the crib, feeling the bars cool and hard on my skin. Mylie's breathing was steadying, but I could still see the shadows of her open eyelids there in the dark.

"It wasn't our Bee Lady who was living there then, of course. It was her grandma. Grandpa Kelly asked Mrs. Quigley if her bees had anything that might fix up Grandpa's leg. Mrs. Quigley took one look at that big old gash, and at Grandpa's face white as cotton fluff, and went right to her shelves for one of her honeys. It was dark and sticky and thick, and when she tipped the jar over Grandpa's leg, it took a long time to roll its slow way out. Mrs. Quigley spread it all over Grandpa's cut with her gentle hands."

Now Mylie's eyes were closed, her little butterfly lashes soft against her cream-colored cheek. I slid my hand off her back and she didn't stir.

"And Grandpa's leg healed so fast and so clean there was hardly even a scar, and he was up and walking by the time the sun set that day," I whispered to myself, and then walked back over to my bed and climbed into it, lying down on top of all my blankets. It was too hot for them, anyway.

It was a true story, that one about Grandpa and his leg. More than once, he'd shown me the thin white line of scar tissue that ran almost from knee to ankle. If there hadn't been a Bee Lady in Maryville, he always said, he probably would've limped through the rest of his life.

I sighed and rolled over. Daddy had gone back into his bedroom while I'd been talking to Mylie, but if I listened real hard, I could still hear those seeds tap-tap-tapping on the kitchen table.

I closed my eyes, trying to forget all about those watermelon seeds, all about Mama yelling and acting worse than she had in a long, long time, wishing there was anything in the world that could pull Mama's brain back together like the skin on Grandpa's leg.

Fixed right up, without anything more than a harmless little scar.

CHAPTER TWO

Mama slept and slept the next morning, all the way through breakfast and then even later. "Just let your mama keep on sleeping," Daddy told me, pulling Mylie's blue church dress over her head. "Think maybe she's coming down with something. You and I can handle church today."

I nodded but didn't say anything, just smooshed my lips together until they burned.

Daddy had just brushed out Mylie's hair and tried to put a little barrette into it to keep the curls out of her face when he realized he didn't have the keys to his truck.

"Della, you seen my key ring?" he asked, his words

clipped little syllables wrapped up in stress. He glanced at the wall clock, ticking its way ever closer to church time.

"No," I said, pausing in the doorway where I was getting ready to take Mylie out and put her into her car seat.

"Darn it all," Daddy muttered, running a hand through his hair so it stuck up all funny. He looked square at Mylie. "Did you take those keys, little monkey?"

It took us nearly ten minutes of combing through the house before we found them, stuck between the couch cushions along with a handful of Cheerios and Mylie's favorite toy, a little plastic phone.

"That dang baby." Daddy grabbed his sunglasses and herded us toward the door and out to the truck.

My best friend, Arden, was the oldest of five kids, but the babies in her family had barely done more than toddle around and giggle when they were sixteen months old. Not Mylie, though. Anybody who knew Mylie knew that she had been born with mischief in her hands and big ideas in her head. Once, Daddy's cell phone had gone missing for most of a day, until I went out to get the eggs and found it in the chicken coop. Another time, she'd stolen Mama's shiny silver credit card, and when a week had gone by without it ever turning up, Mama had

had to spend a whole day on the phone convincing the credit card people to give her another.

"Silly goosey," I whispered as I snapped the car-seat buckles together. She just grinned back. Mylie didn't like a lot of stuff, but she sure liked riding in the car, especially when it was hot summertime and Daddy put the windows down. He put them down today, letting the wind roar over our faces as we bumped down the road toward town.

I sat in the backseat of the pickup and watched the back of Daddy's head. My mouth felt full of words I wasn't saying: Words like *Is Mama really coming down with something, or is it the other thing?* and *Aren't you gonna say something about how she was acting crazy last night, crazy like she used to be?* But all those words stayed right inside my mouth, trapped, through the whole drive to the Maryville Methodist Church. Daddy never liked if I used the word *crazy*, anyway. Said it was unkind and untrue both.

"You're quiet today, Della," he said now, talking loud so I could hear him over the roar of the wind through the open windows. "Come on. Answer me this. Would you rather work seven days at twenty dollars per day, or be paid two dollars for the first day and have your salary double every day for a week?"

"I don't know," I mumbled.

"Well, figure it out."

"It's illegal for a twelve-year-old to have a job anyway."

Daddy's shoulders hunched up just a little. "You're not worrying about your mama, are you? She's gonna be fine, honey. She was just tired last night. Okay, how about this one: Do they have a fourth of July in England?"

"Duh. Of course they do."

"Don't sass," Daddy said, but I could tell he felt bad.

I turned toward the window, resting my chin on my arm and watching the town rush by. Maryville isn't a real town—just a highway that runs through the center, with a bank, a church, a school, and a gas station/convenience store that is the only place to buy food, pump gas, or post mail. Most of Maryville is farms as far as the eye can see, all the way down to the bank of Hummingbird Bay on the Albemarle Sound.

We turned into the church parking lot just before it was time for the service to start. It was hot in the church today, just about as hot as I imagined the devil's place must be. The air-conditioning couldn't keep up with the July heat; all around me, church ladies fanned themselves with programs and wiped limp, sticky hair off their foreheads.

"You wanna take Mylie to the nursery class, Della? I got a car question for Anton," Daddy said when we got there. Anton Jones owned the gas station, and since we didn't have a mechanic, he was the closest thing you could get outside of going to Alberta. I picked Mylie up and hitched her onto my hip, heading off in the direction of the nursery. Her legs and arms were tacky with sweat, like they might stick right to me.

"No!" Mylie started yelling as soon as she saw the door to the nursery class. She kicked her legs back and forth hard, hitting my thighs with her Mary Janes. "No! No! No!"

"It's just your class, Mylie," I said, trying to talk to her like I was her mama and not just her big sister who would really rather be out of this hot church, too. "You love your class. There's Miss Marvella, see?"

"Come on, Mylie honey," Miss Marvella said. "We got lots of fun things to do today."

Mylie's teacher was young and pretty, with light brown skin and long hair braided into cornrows that swayed a little as she waved to us. I'd gone to church a couple times with Grandma and Grandpa Kelly up in Alberta, and most Sundays their service was filled with row after row of sunburned white faces. Maryville was so small—according to the newspaper, the last census had recorded only a couple hundred people—that Maryville Methodist Church was the only church for a half hour's drive, which meant that pretty much anybody Christian ended up there come Sunday morning. I was glad, too; if we'd had white-person churches and black-person churches, like lots of cities did, then Mylie wouldn't have had Miss Marvella for a teacher, which would've been a straight-up disaster. Miss Marvella was just about the only grown-up Mylie liked, aside from my parents and Arden's. During the week she taught kindergarten at the elementary school, and you could tell, because little kids went to her like bees went to the Bee Lady.

But not today. Mylie wasn't having any of it. She arched her back so hard I thought I might drop her, and screamed even louder. "No, NO!"

I put her down before she could fly out of my arms, and she started stamping her feet on the floor like it was covered in ants. Big fat tears were running down her flushed pink cheeks now, splashing onto the collar of her dress and leaving round wet spots. "Wan' Mama," she sobbed, wrapping her arms around my leg so I couldn't move an inch. "Mama, Mama!"

Miss Marvella bent down, trying to pry Mylie's arms off me. "Your mama not feeling well, sugar?" she asked, her voice quiet, like she was talking to a skittish horse.

"You wanna come play with me and the others now? You gone be just fine, sweet baby."

Mylie just cried harder, pressing her face into my leg until I could feel the tears seeping through my own dress.

I sighed. "She can just come with us today," I said, reaching down to pull Mylie's head away from my skirt. "You hear that, silly baby? You can come with Della and Daddy, okay? But you gotta stop crying and you gotta stay quiet the *whole* time."

Mylie stopped crying so fast she choked, gagging on her own tears.

"You sure?" Miss Marvella asked.

"We'll be all right," I said to Miss Marvella, and then looked down at Mylie. "You come on, little monster. And be *quiet*."

After the service was over we got stopped by church lady after church lady, all of them waving their fans and asking about Mama. "She doin' all right?" "Can I bring you a meal tonight?" "Suzanne be needing help with the kids this week? I know that baby is a handful and a half." Daddy and I just shook our heads and smiled real big, saying, "No, thank you" over and over.

"Suzie's just feeling a little under the weather," Daddy said, keeping a firm hold on Mylie's hand so she couldn't dash off through the open church doors and into the parking lot. It wouldn't have been the first time. "She'll be back to her usual self by tomorrow, I'm sure of it. We'll be just fine, but thanks for the offer."

"You just call me anytime y'all need anything at all," they all said, one after another, their husbands nodding agreement. Each one of them church ladies looked hard into my eyes, like they were checking to see if Daddy was telling the truth or not. I did my best to smile big and normal, trying not to think about the night before.

The image of Mama with a watermelon seed stuck above her eyebrow was burned right into me.

I wished Arden were there. She was the kind of person who wasn't afraid to talk to anyone and knew just how to make other people smile. That was one of the reasons that I was pretty sure even if we hadn't grown up seeing each other nearly every day, I'd still have wanted to be her best friend. Being with Arden made it okay that I was quiet, okay that sometimes I blushed around new people and stumbled over my words.

If Arden had been there, she would've given me the courage to go back home and see how Mama was doing this morning. But the Hawthornes were one of the few families in town that didn't go to church on Sundays; it was just one more thing that made people raise their eyebrows when they thought Arden's parents weren't looking. Everybody in Maryville loved the Hawthornes, but most everybody also agreed they were just a little *different.*

I always figured that Maryville could use all the *different* it could get.

We were almost out the door and into the bright-white summer sunlight when one last church lady caught us, her pale light-blond hair shining in the sun. She was only medium-old for an adult, not much older than my daddy, but she was the kind of grown-up who spoke so confidently and knew so much that she might have been alive a hundred years.

It was Miss Tabitha Quigley. The Bee Lady.

She had a backyard full of white beehives, the bees buzzing around them till the whole place hummed with it, and her honey wasn't just the kind you could get from any grocery store. It was pretty well accepted that the Bee Lady's honey could cheer you up if you were feeling down, or fix your broken heart, or help you see things clearer when you had big decisions to make. Some people even mixed her honey into water and poured it on their gardens and farms, swearing it made their plants grow twice as strong.

"Noticed y'all all alone in your pew today," Miss Tabitha said. Her eyes were the same bright blue as the silky turquoise scarf she wore, so blue it looked like they couldn't possibly be real. Mama said the Quigleys had always had those eyes, as far back as anyone in town could remember. Even here inside the church building, a black-and-gold bee darted back and forth above her, its wings like lace in the light from the glass doors. Miss Tabitha didn't seem to notice it.

"Hi there, Tabitha. Suzanne's just feeling a little under the weather," said Daddy, looking out the doorway to where his truck sat parked, invisible in the haze from the heat and the sun. "Just got a little one of them summer colds."

"Sorry to hear that," said Miss Tabitha, putting a pale hand down on my shoulder in that absentminded way grown-ups sometimes did. Her skin smelled like honey and lavender.

"Thanks," said Daddy, with a grimace that was probably meant to look like a smile.

"You tell me if you ever need anything, Della, you hear?" Her voice was as warm and soft as her skin, as sweet as the honey she sold.

I looked up at her, my tongue all tied up in knots. I'd always felt a little shy around the Bee Lady—even more shy than I felt around most folks. Seeing her was like seeing somebody step right out of the stories that Mama used to tell to me, the stories I loved to tell Mylie. Plenty of people had a little bit of magic to them, but the Quigleys and their bees had more than most.

Standing there in that light-and-shadow entryway, I wanted to open my mouth so bad and tell her everything that had happened the night before, wanted to beg her to give me some of her magic honey to fix Mama up like Miss Tabitha's grandma had once fixed Grandpa Kelly's leg.

But Daddy was standing right there beside me, his hand in Mylie's, impatience written all over his face, and I knew if I said anything it would only frustrate him more. I knew without even asking that he didn't want anyone to know about Mama right now, didn't want anyone hearing about how she'd been with the watermelon seeds last night, didn't want anyone putting two and two together.

"It's important for your mama to have dignity, Della," he'd told me more than once, his eyes sad. "And lots of people, they don't understand an illness like your mama's, like schizophrenia. They hear that name and start to use hurtful words, like 'crazy' and 'psychotic,' and start seeing a person as just a disease, not a human being. Your mama's always going to have good days and bad days, and we'll get through them the way we always have. Together, as a family."

Daddy figured that since schizophrenia had been part of our family exactly as long as I had, nobody knew as well as we did how to handle it. And maybe I'd felt that way, too, sometimes.

But not right now. Not after last night. Those watermelon seeds had been something worse, something more than all Mama's symptoms since the bad time.

I could see just the way Daddy's mouth would pull together into a thin line if he heard me beg magic honey off Miss Tabitha.

Don't go bothering Miss Quigley, he'd say, holding on to Mylie's hand while she tried to tug him toward the car. *You know just as well as I do, Della, that your mama's medication is the best treatment available.*

But what Daddy didn't understand was that after last night, *treatment* didn't feel like enough. *Treatment* meant "good days and bad days."

What I wanted was a *cure*—not something that would work for just a year or two at a time, like Mama's medicines. Something that would heal *forever*, so we never had to worry again.

CHAPTER THREE

Mama was awake when we got home from church, acting like her regular old self and slicing up bread for lunchtime sandwiches. Mylie ran right up to her and wrapped her arms around Mama's legs, whimpering like she might start crying again.

"Hush, honey," said Mama. "I'll pick you up just as soon as I'm done here. Della, you want to find some play clothes for Mylie to wear? I don't want her eating lunch in her nice Sunday dress."

I watched Mama real close, not moving. She looked pretty, in a pair of shorts and a tank top, with her straw-colored hair pulled up into a ponytail. She was done slicing bread now and was working on the mayo, spreading it fast over all the pieces she'd cut and then slapping ham on top of it. She seemed perfectly, perfectly normal.

Mama looked up and caught me watching. "Didn't you hear what I said, Della? Go find some play clothes for Mylie to wear—quick now, because I'm almost done with these sandwiches!"

The phone rang just as we were all finishing up our lunch, and Daddy got it. "Hi there, Mama. Hi, Daddy," he said, and tucked the phone between his shoulder and his neck and started washing up our sandwich plates while he talked. Grandma and Grandpa Kelly called most Sunday afternoons; they'd lived with us for nearly my whole entire life, until Grandpa had a stroke last fall and his doctor told him he had to stop farming and move closer to the hospital. Grandpa cussed up a blue streak, but Grandma put her foot down, and they moved into a house in Alberta only a few weeks later.

I missed having them around, but I liked it, too, since it meant that Mylie and I got to move into a real true bedroom for the first time ever. When Grandma and Grandpa lived with us, Mylie had slept in with Mama and Daddy, and I had a tiny little bed in an old storage room Daddy had painted pink when I turned two.

I handed Daddy my plate and started putting away

the lemonade pitcher and the sandwich fixings. Mama had got up from the table already and taken Mylie in for a nap, but I didn't think it was working, since all I could hear from my bedroom was hollering and banging, like Mylie was kicking the crib the way she did when she didn't want to go to sleep.

"Mm-hmm," Daddy said into the phone handset. I could hear Grandma's voice through it, tinny and garbled like it was coming from a million miles away, even though Alberta was just a little more than an hour in the truck. "Yep, that sounds real nice." Daddy closed the dishwasher and wiped his wet hands off on a towel. "Glad they're taking good care of you, Mama. What's that?" Now the voice spilling out of the receiver was Grandpa's deep and husky one. Grandpa's voice sounded like his skin looked—suntanned and weathered, a little dry and a little crackly.

Daddy's lips pulled tight into a line. I kept sneaking looks at him out of the corner of my eye as I cleaned the table with a wet rag, curiosity boiling up my throat like water. "The farm's fine. Nope, everything's just fine, Dad. Yeah, the drought's pretty bad, but it's not hurting the crops too much. Costing us a bit more in water, but we'll be okay. Yeah, Suzie's great. No problems at all."

I stopped bothering to hide my eavesdropping and

stared at Daddy. *No problems at all?*

"Here, Della," Daddy said, turning and reaching the phone out toward me. "Give me that rag and take this. Grandma has something she wants to tell you."

I took the handset from him and put it to my ear. "Della honey," said Grandma through the phone, "I found a recipe yesterday that made me think of you." Grandma's words were always like slow, sweet syrup, and no matter what she was saying, listening to her always made me feel better. Grandma grew up in Georgia before she married Grandpa, and you could still hear that Georgia sun in every word she said. "Watermelon limeade. Bet you'd like that, wouldn't you, sweetheart? Soon as I saw it, I said to your granddaddy, 'I gotta send that to our little watermelon girl.' I'm gonna email it to you this afternoon, before I forget."

"Sounds delicious. Love you, Grandma."

"Love you, too, Della. Tell your mama and Mylie hi for us. Bye, shug."

I put the phone back on its cradle just as my bedroom door opened and Mama came out. Mylie was quiet now, so I guessed she must have gone to sleep, after all. I opened my mouth to tell Mama about Grandma's recipe, but the words died before they made it up to my tongue.

Mama wasn't looking at me—wasn't looking at anything. Still, her head was nodding over and over again, just like mine had when Grandma was telling me about the watermelon limeade. Just like Mama was having a conversation with somebody the rest of us couldn't see at all.

CHAPTER FOUR

Monday morning, seeing Arden felt like running through a sprinkler on a hot day.

Every day of the week except Sunday, the two of us met in the morning to take a shift at the farm stand our families ran together, selling melons and berries and peaches and whatever else was in season to tourists who drove up and down the highway, on their way to places that were more interesting than Maryville. Sometimes people asked if we were sisters or twins, since we both had light skin, brown hair, and brown eyes. Those questions always felt like a little warm light had been turned on inside my heart. Arden may not have been my sister for real, but most of the time, she felt like something just as good.

The farm stand was simple, just a big canvas canopy held up by four metal poles with a cement pad underneath. The Kelly farm had had something or other here for longer than Daddy had been alive, but he and Mr. Ben had made it nicer, pouring the cement when me and Arden were just a few years old. You could still see our chubby little toddler handprints in a corner, where our daddies had pressed our hands into the wet cement and written our names and the date underneath. The farm stand was as much a part of me as the farm itself, or the bay, or the sound of cicadas on a hot summer night.

Business was quiet today, only a few tourists stopping by to fill their trunks. When we didn't have any customers, Arden and I sat cross-legged on the ground, a bucket of sidewalk chalk between us.

We were probably too old to play with chalk like little kids, but ever since our obsession with *Mary Poppins* when we were seven, we'd spent every summer trying to draw a mural realistic enough to step into. They didn't last very long—between the thunderstorms that visited Maryville most summer afternoons so long as we weren't in a drought, and the wind that blew the chalk dust away, the pictures were usually gone within a day or two. Once, Arden had looked it up on the computer and figured out that real sidewalk artists spray hairspray on top to make the drawings last longer, but we never had. There was only space on the farm stand floor for a couple murals at a time. It was more fun to let them fade and create something brand-new a few days later.

Sometimes we took pictures of our favorites, though. If we asked her to, Miss Amanda would print them off for us, and Arden and I would pick through them and choose the best ones to hang up on the walls of our bedrooms. During the bad time when I was eight, while Mama was getting sicker and sicker, I used to lie on my bed and look at those prints and imagine that if I tried hard enough, I could Mary Poppins my way right into those pictures and disappear into a life made out of color and fun.

Today we were sketching out two halves of a sun: Arden using a chalk the color of Daddy's wheat when it's ripe, me with one just the same shade as the summer sky. Where our colors met in the middle, I'd traced a swirling line. Right now I was filling in the shadows on my side of the sun's face, using navy and gray to make it look like that two-colored sun was ready to send its warmth right off the sidewalk.

"That looks kind of depressing," Arden said with a corner-of-the-eye glance at me.

"What do you mean?" I asked, sitting back on my heels to look at it. I wasn't the world's best artist, but after so many years of practicing, we were both pretty good. And I liked drawing. The two things in the world I was best at were math problems and telling stories, and drawing is a little bit of both. Our yellow-blue sun, even only halfway done, pulled at something deep inside me, like one of the curling rays that wrapped around its center had hooked into me somewhere behind my belly button.

"I don't know. It's just kind of sad, isn't it? Like it's cheerful over here, and depressed over there."

"I like it." What I didn't know how to say was that I liked it *because* of that, because of the way the happiness and the sadness swirled together in the middle, two halves of a whole. This week, I couldn't have drawn with yellow if I'd tried.

I rubbed my thumb against the gray chalk in my hand.

Arden has been my best friend since before I was even born, when my mama was right at the end of her pregnancy and Miss Amanda brought baby Arden over (*All wrapped up in some big sheet, like a baby kangaroo*, my mama always says) to say hello. They'd moved down from Boston and bought the farm just east of us, wanting to "live closer to the land" and "build a sustainable lifestyle" (says my mama with her fingers scrunched into little quotation marks).

Mama and Daddy were sure they'd wash out and move back north before long. Both Arden's parents have fancy degrees and had big-city jobs before they moved down south, and Mama and Daddy figured they wouldn't be cut out for the never-ending hard work and not much money you get out of running a farm. But they stayed, and now none of us can imagine what life would be like without them as neighbors. The Hawthornes sure cause a lot of talking over the fence from everyone in Maryville, even now, but Mr. Ben and Miss Amanda are both so sweet and kind I don't think you could find a single soul in town who didn't like them despite it all.

"You okay? How's Miss Suzanne?" Even in Mama's good moments, people still asked about her.

"Yeah." I itched to tell Arden everything, but I was scared, too. Maybe I hadn't all the way agreed with Daddy about not telling anybody about the watermelon seeds the day before, but I still understood. Sometimes, if I talked too much about Mama and her hard times, that was all people asked about—they'd look at us and see a *sad family with big problems*. And then they'd worry, and ask me about Mama every time I saw them. And they'd go around treating me and Mama and Daddy and even

Mylie like we were made out of glass, ready to shatter any second.

Still, the memory of Saturday night—and of the way Mama had been hearing voices in her head nobody else could hear yesterday—was rising up in me the way a balloon fills with air, making my skin tight and stretched.

A dizzy-looking honeybee bumbled its way past my head, twirling over the produce boxes toward the wildflowers that bloomed tall beside the highway. I thought of the Bee Stories, of the question that had been on the tip of my tongue when I'd seen Miss Tabitha the day before.

"I have to tell you what happened this weekend," I started, squeezing my chalk so hard the edges of it crumbled in my hand.

"Oh yeah." Arden giggled. "That reminds me—I was going to tell you something about the weekend, too. But you first," she added loyally, blending white chalk through one of her streaming yellow sunbeams.

The little bubble of courage inside me popped.

"Never mind. You go ahead." Even best friends get it wrong sometimes—I couldn't blame Arden for not being able to read my mind, not being able to sense just how much I *needed* to talk about what had happened. But that one breath of being brave was over, and all my words were stuck in me just as deeply as they had been since Saturday night. I swallowed hard and went back to drawing.

"So, Mom has been saying that Eli's room smelled funny for at least a week now," Arden said. "She's made him clean it twice but still thought something was strange in there. Eli has promised over and over that there's nothing in there that shouldn't be."

Slowly, listening to Arden tell her story, the strings wound around my heart loosened up a little. If I tried hard enough, I could even forget the image of Mama Saturday night with a watermelon seed above her eye.

Mostly.

"Then last night, Dad went in there to ask Eli something and he heard a noise. Coming from the closet." Arden's nose scrunched up in remembered humor. "I was in the kitchen loading the dishwasher and Mom was putting the little girls to bed, and all of a sudden we all heard a shriek from Eli, and Dad shouting, 'YOU HAVE A FROG LIVING IN YOUR CLOSET?!'"

Arden was all the way laughing now, her swirling yellow sun-half forgotten on the pavement in front of her. "So it turned out that Eli found this tree frog down by Hummingbird Bay last week and decided to keep it. So he put it in a shoe box and he's been catching crickets and ants to feed it ever since."

I laughed without even meaning to. Eli was Arden's ten-year-old brother, and it'd been war between the two of them for just about as long as they'd been alive. The picture of him sneaking bugs into his closet, a little brown frog hiding unhappily in a dark shoe box, was just like him.

"What did your parents do?" I asked.

"Oh, they were furious. Mom gave him a big lecture on respect for life and caring properly for living creatures."

"Did they make him take it back outside?"

"Nah. Dad dug out an old aquarium and helped Eli build it a habitat. Said as long as the frog is healthy, he can stay. Eli named it Bartholomew."

I brushed my palms together again and again until they were mostly free of chalk dust. That was the only part of drawing I didn't like—the way the grit stayed on my skin, hiding deep in the cracks and crevices of my hands, until I washed them good with soap. All the way completed, our yellow-and-blue sun didn't look sad at all to me anymore. It just looked *real*. Good and bad. Sad and happy. Worrying and laughing.

Kind of like today.

"What was it you wanted to tell me?" Arden asked.

"Nothing," I said. And I meant it. Somehow that little bit of laughter and silliness had cleared the air inside of me.

A ladybug flitted down to land on the top of my hand. Ladybugs were always around me and Arden—lucky ladybugs, Mama called them, and laughed that it was a part of the magic Arden and I made together. When Arden and I are together, things all around us know it—when it's our turn to sell at the stand, the fruit is riper and shinier, the herbs smell sweeter, the cut flower bouquets from our mamas' gardens hold little warbles of birdsong caught in their petals.

I blew the ladybug gently off.

Arden sat up. There was a big streak of orange chalk across her white cheek. "Do you ever think what would've happened if my mom and dad hadn't decided to move down here?"

I shuddered. "Don't even say that. It would've been awful." I've got other friends at school, when school's in session, but nobody at all like Arden, who knows me better than I know my own self.

Arden stuck out her hand, all the fingers folded down except for her pinkie. "Best friends forever?"

"Forever," I agreed, wrapping my pinkie around hers and giving it a firm shake. It was our promise, the one we'd been making for as long as I could remember.

"Wanna get Popsicles when we're done?"

"Sure. It's hot enough." I tossed the chalk I'd been using into the chalk bucket. The thump it made was echoed a minute later by a much louder *thump-thump, thump-thump,* and a cloud of dust moved down Arden's driveway with Mr. Ben's old rusted-out pickup in the middle of it.

"Finally!" Arden said, standing up and stretching. Arden is about my same size, but she can run so fast her feet have trouble staying on the ground, so she looks athletic while I just look soft in some places and bony in others.

Mr. Ben parked beside the pavilion and jumped down from the truck, waving at us. He had a big straw hat on, casting his pale face into shadow. "You girls ready for a break?"

"*Yes,*" said Arden. "Can we bike to Mr. Anton's to get some Popsicles or something?"

"That's fine with me," said Mr. Ben, checking the record of the couple of transactions we'd made that morning, "but Della will need to ask her parents."

Arden shaded her eyes and looked off across the highway, toward my place. "Is that your dad over there, Dell?"

Daddy's truck was rumbling toward us from the direction of my house, kicking up a cloud of dust just like Mr. Ben's had a moment ago, one more reminder of the drought that wouldn't let Maryville go.

"Hoped it was your turn over here, Ben," Daddy said, after he'd parked and jumped out of the truck cab into the shade of the pavilion. "Wanna pick your brain. Something's turning my watermelon leaves brown and it's got me worrying." He sighed. "Just what I need on top of everything else. We've been going dawn to dusk every day for the last few weeks trying to get the wheat in."

"Daddy, can Arden and I bike over to the gas station and get Popsicles?"

"Actually, I need to go gas up," Daddy said. "You girls go on along and hop in the truck and get the AC cranking, and I'll be right along." He tossed his keys over to me, silver in the hot summer sun.

"I'm starting to think making all these changes was a bad idea," Daddy was saying to Mr. Ben as Arden and I climbed up into Daddy's truck. "Seems like it's all turning into a disaster. The Kelly farm has been ours since my great-granddaddy's time, Ben, and I can't imagine trying to look my own daddy in the eye if I lost it."

"Well, anything I can do to help, you just ask," Mr.

Ben said. "Sorry for the stress. Suzanne doing okay?"

Daddy paused with his hand on the driver's-side door. "Well," he said, each of his words as carefully picked as the strawberries we sold in the spring, "she's got her ups and downs, just like always. But we're doing fine."

CHAPTER FIVE

It's almost a mile from our stand to the gas station and Duck-Thru Food Store, owned by Mr. Anton Jones. Mr. Anton is about as tall as a tree, with great big reddish-brown hands that are always stained with gasoline or motor oil. He's one of the nicest grown-ups in town, and usually has a little treat for me and Mylie whenever we go with Daddy to gas up.

Arden and I climbed out as Daddy pulled the truck around to one of the gas pumps. A black boy I'd never seen before, maybe sixteen or seventeen, stood on the curb by the gas station, sinking the pole of what looked like the world's strangest birdhouse into the dirt that ran between the parking lot and the highway. The birdhouse was bigger than the boy's head, with a glass door and a shelf inside it, and no matter how hard I looked, I couldn't figure out how the birds would get into it. Arden and I watched him for a long minute, neither of us brave enough to ask what he was doing.

Finally, he looked up and saw us. His smile was like the first time you glimpse a seedling coming up from the ground—bright and happy and made me feel happy, too, just seeing it. His eyes were the color of a crayon I'd had once called *umber*, such a deep, rich brown it felt like I might get dizzy just looking at them.

"Mornin', ladies," he said, and came over and stuck out his hand for us to shake, just like we were all grown up. His accent was a lot lighter than most folks in Maryville; Miss Amanda, who was from Boston and talked like she was holding her nose closed, said that the Maryville accent was "thick enough to stuff pillows." The new boy talked more like Arden: halfway between North and South, some words sharp and some words twanging.

Arden glanced up, her eyes squinting against the sunlight. "It's more like afternoon now."

The stranger laughed. "Guess you're about right. My name's Thomas Bradley. Anton's my uncle. Me and my mama just moved into town last night."

"I'm Arden Hawthorne. This is Della Kelly, though I guess she forgot how to talk."

"Did not," I said, but I said it quietly. "What are you putting up over there?"

"It's a library," said Thomas, and I couldn't keep my jaw from dropping down just a little. Maryville might not have a library of its own, but I'd been to the library in Windsor plenty of times, and it was a lot bigger than a birdhouse.

Thomas smiled. "A little library. A box library, I guess. Or it will be, once it's got some books in it."

Just then, the bell over Mr. Anton's shop door jingled and a woman came out, Mr. Anton walking beside her. Both of their arms were filled with books.

"See?" Thomas said. "Here come the books now. This is my mama, Lorena Bradley. Mama, this is Arden here, and Della." Thomas took the stack of books from his mama and lined them all up neat and tidy in the box library.

"I confess I wasn't very happy about moving to a town where you've gotta drive nearly half an hour to get to a library," Mrs. Bradley said. She was younger than Mr. Anton, with warm brown skin and tight curls that reached to her chin and looked touched with amber in the sunlight, and when she said that bit about the library being so far away, she gave a sly little grin in Mr. Anton's direction.

He chuckled. "Took me quite a while to convince my baby sister to come live here in the middle of nowhere. She and her boy, they're city folk from up Norfolk way." He wrapped an arm around Mrs. Bradley's shoulders and squeezed. "I finally wore 'em down. It'll be nice, having some company in that lonely old house."

Mrs. Bradley patted the book box. "This was my way of making myself feel a bit better about the library situation. Thomas built it for me."

"But how does it work?" I asked, my voice timid in my own ears. My face heated, and it wasn't just from the sun beating down on us all.

"It's an honor system," said Thomas. "Anyone who wants can take a book out or put one in. It's not a real library, but it might have something different than what you've already got at home."

"Would you like to look at what we've got in there now, sugar?" Mrs. Bradley asked, looking at me with eyes that seemed to see all the way into my bones.

"My favorites are these," Thomas said, tapping the books at one end. There were three of them, each one thick, with pages that were all ruffled, like they had been read lots. "*The Lord of the Rings*. I just got new copies, so I figured I'd donate these here."

"They're kind of . . . long," I whispered.

"Go on," said Mrs. Bradley. "Look what else we have."

The box library smelled like sawdust and sunlight, and the glass door was heavy on its smooth hinges as I opened it wider, so I could see everything in there. I had to turn my head sideways to read all the titles—some I'd seen before or even read in school, like *The Crossover*, and some I'd never heard of, like *Akata Witch*. My favorite was a tiny little book with a sky-colored spine that just said *POEMS* in big letters and *Emily Dickinson* in small ones. I put up a finger and touched it, tentative as a feather. The jacket was cool and soft.

"Y'all going to get those Popsicles?" Daddy asked, coming up behind Mr. Anton and Mrs. Bradley.

"Yeah," I said, not wanting to let the book go.

"You wanna take that with you, Della?" Mrs. Bradley asked.

Without even meaning to, I slipped the book out of the box library and held it in my hands, looking down at it. "Yes," I whispered, and then cleared my throat.

"I mean, yes, ma'am, Mrs. Bradley," I said again, louder this time. "If that's all right, I'd like to borrow it. When do I gotta bring it back?" Mama and I used to drive to the library plenty, but we hadn't been a single time since Mylie was born. I didn't read anywhere near as much as Mama did, but something about having a brand-new book I'd never seen before wrapped up in my arms felt like coming home.

"Please, go on ahead and call me Miss Lorena. Bring it back whenever you're done. There's no hurry. And if you find you want to keep it, just bring us another one to trade."

"Thank you, ma'am. I'll be fast, I promise."

"No need," said Miss Lorena, smiling. I could see where Thomas got his springtime smile from; Miss Lorena's liked to light up the whole town. "You take your time, honey—that one's an especially good one."

"By the way," Daddy said, sticking his hand out for Miss Lorena and then Thomas to shake it. "I'm Miles Kelly. Della's daddy. Anton mentioned yesterday he had family coming to stay—I guess that's you two?"

Miss Lorena nodded.

"Actually, Miles," said Mr. Anton, clapping a hand on Thomas's back. "Remember how you was telling me you might be on the lookout for some help this summer? I imagine there's not many kids around here who aren't busy helping their own daddies. But Thomas mentioned last night he'd be looking for a summer job."

"I can't say I know a single blessed thing about farm

work," Thomas said, "but I'm game to give it a try."

"You sure?" Daddy asked.

"It'd keep him out of trouble this summer," Miss Lorena said with a grin.

"Probably four or five days a week," said Daddy. "Mostly mornings. You could start tomorrow, if you like. Anton knows my address."

"Cool," said Thomas. "I'll see you then, Mr. Kelly. And you too, probably, Della," he added, looking right at me.

I hugged the Emily Dickinson book to me, feeling it hard against my chest just like a second heart, and tried not to let my cheeks flame as red as the cherry tomatoes dripping off the vines in the garden out behind our house.

CHAPTER SIX

That whole week was just about the hottest I'd ever lived through. Every day Daddy came in from the fields looking like he'd been dunked in a swimming pool. Thomas had come by to help one morning, too, and even though he didn't say anything, I could tell by the look in his dark eyes when he came in to get a cold drink that he'd never worked that hard or been that hot in his life. Still, he didn't complain, even if he downed that sweet tea like it was the best thing he'd ever tasted.

By Thursday night I felt like I couldn't remember a time when I hadn't been sticky and salty, my hair clinging to my skin all around my head till I wanted to cut it as short as Daddy's just to give me some relief. In every room we had ceiling fans and big box fans and little tiny round fans working as hard as they could, and it still wasn't ever enough.

It would've been better if we'd had the AC going, too, but our unit had broken in May and Mama refused to let a repairman come out to look at it.

"Why in the Sam Hill not?" Daddy had asked when she'd stopped him calling the air-conditioning company.

"I just don't think we should run it right now, Miles," Mama had said, holding his phone behind her back so he couldn't make the call. "It's got all those chemicals in it—just think of the ways it could hurt our girls. The fans are better. We got along fine without the AC for years and years, didn't we?"

Daddy had gaped at her for a minute but then laughed. "You are the strangest woman alive," he'd said to Mama, and then kissed her on the lips. I'd tried hard to forget I'd heard the conversation at all, even though it was impossible to do once the heat set in. I never liked noticing the ways that Mama was different. Mama had always worried about me and Mylie, probably more than most mothers. But it had never been as bad as last Saturday night, with Mama sitting in the ghostly light of the fridge, picking seeds out of watermelons.

That afternoon the temperature had hit 105, which

was a record high for Maryville and nearly everywhere around us, too.

"I can practically hear the crops drying up and dying out there in the fields," Daddy told Mama, his voice flat as rolled-out pie dough, while I was weeding in the big garden. I squinted in the sunlight as I picked; Mylie had stolen my sunglasses earlier that morning, and for the life of me I couldn't figure out where she'd put them.

Mama and Daddy had both spent all of Mylie's nap time working outside, Daddy driving the combine to finish up the July harvest of winter wheat and Mama picking boxes full of tomatoes to sell at the stand. We'd got so behind on everything this month that lots of the tomatoes had swelled and split down the middle, turning to mush right on their plants so they were good for nothing but the compost heap. Now Mama and Daddy stood by the tractor, Daddy twisting his baseball cap over in his work-tanned hands.

"It's getting to be the only thing I can think about, Suzie. We're not set up for this much summer irrigation, and everything's suffering for it. At this point I'll be grateful if we just break even this year. It's not looking likely."

"We'll make ends meet somehow," Mama said.

"I sure hope so." But when Mama turned to go back

inside, *hopeful* wasn't exactly the look on Daddy's face.

The heat didn't make any of us happy, but Mylie was the worst. She was never much of a one for going to bed, but lately she'd been pitching more fits than ever, probably because it felt like an oven inside our room. Most nights Daddy put her to bed, but Thursdays were special, and Mama took over bedtime so that Daddy and I could watch our favorite detective show together. We'd been watching TV mysteries nearly since I got old enough to talk, and we always had a competition to see who could solve them first. Daddy usually won, but I was getting better these days and beat him plenty.

Mysteries were a little like math. When all the pieces slotted together in my head, it felt just like solving a problem and *knowing* I'd got it right, the way everything inside me suddenly snapped into perfect order.

Tonight Mylie was still screaming her head off when our show started, and I turned it up real loud so we could hear it.

"Turn it down, Della," said Daddy, rubbing his forehead so hard it looked more pink than tan. "The noise'll just keep Mylie up longer. Put on the captions instead."

I huffed out a sigh and did as he asked. Mylie cried so loud through the first half of the show that I could hardly even read the subtitles, my thoughts were so jumbled, but she finally quieted down just as the cops put the wrong person in jail and a commercial started.

Mama stomped out of my bedroom, looking like a wild woman with her hair all jammed up into a ponytail and sweaty wisps plastered to her forehead.

"I tell you, I *cannot* take the sass of that child anymore," she said, going into the kitchen and pouring herself a big glass of ice-cold filtered water from the refrigerator. Mama never drank water from the tap, only from her special pitcher with the filter in it to keep all the bad stuff out.

Daddy muted the TV and turned to look at Mama. "Sorry she was so hard, Suzie. Wanna come finish the show with us?"

Mama sat down on the sofa next to him, the water sloshing quietly in her glass. She closed her eyes and let out a big, long breath. "I'm just so tired of fighting with her over every little dumb thing. She's not even a year and a half. Isn't that way too young for this? Della never had a tantrum till she was at least three."

Daddy put his hand around Mama's shoulder and gave her a squeeze. "Nothing lasts forever," he said, unmuting the TV as our show came back on. "This won't, either."

Mylie stayed asleep all the way through the rest of the show, but Mama got shiftier and shiftier, her eyes getting wide and her fingers twisting together as she watched. Just a few minutes before it finished up, I put all the clues together and came up with an answer I was sure was right—but before I could open my mouth to beat Daddy to the solution, Mama pointed at the screen.

"It's the social worker," she said, looking queasy. "She was the only one who wasn't with them that night, right? And she had access to all those files."

Right as she finished talking, the detectives on the television came to the same conclusion.

Daddy looked at Mama with his eyebrows up, smiling. "Nice job, Suzie," he said. Mama almost never played our game; she just liked to watch, she said, and have a chance to rest like she never could during the day. "I was miles away from that. I'm impressed."

I clapped my mouth shut as the credits started to roll. That had been *my* guess, too.

"Wasn't hard. But I don't like this show," Mama said, pressing her lips together till they turned white. "Don't want Della watching it no more. That woman was hurting a little girl, just like people keep on trying to hurt my girls."

"What do you mean?" Daddy asked, reaching over to hit the power button on the remote, his voice like a cliff-edge walk—just a breath away from getting really, really upset.

"My daddy keeps telling me, Miles. He keeps on telling me there are people out there wanting to hurt Mylie and Della."

The only sound in the whole house was the *whir-whir-whir* of half a dozen fans, blades rotating around and around so fast they became invisible. Daddy and I both stared.

Mama's daddy, my grandpa Case, died of a heart attack when I was eight years old.

"Suzanne, honey," said Daddy at the breakfast table the next morning. He wasn't looking at Mama—he was looking down at the butter he was spreading across his biscuit instead. His words were careful and slow, like soldiers creeping into enemy territory. "I made you an appointment with Dr. DuBose for later this morning, okay? It's been awhile since you been to see him. I can drive you there, if you like."

"You what?" asked Mama, jaw tightening. "I haven't got time today, Miles. Who'd watch Mylie and Della?"

"I don't need watching," I said. "And I could stay with Mylie. Or we could go to Miss Amanda's."

Mama kept on like I was no louder than a fly buzzing round the kitchen. "And what do you mean, you'd drive me there? There's no way you could take the day off chores today, not with this drought. And if I drove myself, what would you do all on your own? In case you haven't noticed, I've been spending a whole lot of time out on the farm lately."

"I know, Suzie, thanks for that." Daddy rubbed at his forehead. Mylie picked her sippy cup up experimentally and launched it at Mama's head; Mama caught it and put it back on the tray without even looking up.

"Never thought I'd say this, but I miss having my parents here. Things seemed to run a little smoother around here with four adults instead of just two. Still," Daddy added after a moment, his voice quieter than ever. "I think you ought to take that appointment. We can leave the girls here—I'll call Amanda and tell her to keep an eye on them. It could be nice, Suzie, having some time just for the two of us. Thomas is coming in a bit. He can handle a few chores by himself for one morning."

"Honestly," said Mama, sounding about ready to take Daddy's head off with one bite. "*I'm fine.* Actually, I've been feeling more like myself than I have since Mylie was born. Nothing's wrong with me, and I don't need to go wasting Dr. DuBose's time or my own. And besides, last I checked, there's twice as many of those squash beetles out there—and if we don't get weeding done out in your vegetable field, the seed heads'll start popping and we'll be in a world of trouble—"

"I'm not saying anything's wrong with you. Just that you haven't been to see him in a long time. Won't you be running out of pills soon? When does your prescription expire?"

"Not for months. Now finish shredding that biscuit and stop bugging me."

After we'd finished eating, Daddy took his keys down off their hook by the door and went outside. The pickup engine rumbled to life, but either Mama didn't notice or she was ignoring that sound as hard as she could.

I closed my eyes and thought of numbers. *One. Two. Four. Eight. Sixteen.*

Half an hour later, Thomas Bradley's blue car pulled into the driveway. Daddy gave up and turned the truck engine off.

"Hey, Della, how you doing?" Thomas called, waving as he and Daddy passed through the house to the back door, which was the quickest way to get to the fields.

Daddy didn't even look at me. His face was hard, stormy as one of the rain clouds we hadn't seen all summer long.

CHAPTER SEVEN

After we'd finished our shift at the farm stand that morning, Arden and I escaped down to our playhouse. We'd built it last summer, right by where the curve of Hummingbird Bay met the edge of the Hawthorne farm, and both our daddies hated it because we'd made it ourselves out of old plywood we scavenged from the supplies my daddy used to build our chicken coop last year. Before that we'd spent years playing in an old tobacco shed, but the playhouse was better, because it was made with our own hands.

Mr. Ben said it was unsafe and would fall over on us next time a hurricane rolled through town, but Arden always shot back that we didn't plan to stay in the playhouse during a hurricane, so that wouldn't be a problem.

The playhouse was *our* place, the one place in Maryville where nobody could come unless we let them. Today Arden had all her younger siblings to watch except the baby, but the three of them were busy down at the water's edge trying to catch tadpoles and water skimmers in nets, so Arden and I got the playhouse to ourselves as long as we kept a good eye on them. We were painting the walls with paints and brushes we'd snuck out of Arden's mama's craft room, trying to make it look as much like a real house as a rickety plywood box nailed together by two eleven-year-olds can. Arden wanted to paint the whole thing over with flowers once we'd finished with the base coat, but I hadn't decided what I thought yet. The idea of making something that permanent, the kind of thing you couldn't just wash off and start over, made me nervous.

"Eli!" Arden yelled, looking up from her painting to see her brother wading into the bay so far his shorts got wet. Eli hated being bossed. "Get out of the water! Mom said no swimming unless she or Dad are with us."

Arden and I went swimming in there without any grown-ups all the time, dunking each other under the brackish water or trying to swim all the way out to the point where the bay opened up into the Albemarle Sound, but nobody else but us knew about that.

Eli stuck out his tongue at us, but he obeyed, trudging back to the shore with his skinny white legs dripping water.

"I can't believe summer's nearly half over." Arden sounded wistful.

"Me neither." I'd always been shy, and every new school year was like jumping back into a cold pool once you've finally warmed up. Seventh grade had to be better than sixth—starting at a new school was worse than almost anything—but I still wasn't looking forward to it. The seventh graders last year had seemed so old, so smart, so mysterious. There had been whispers about kissing and boyfriends and things I didn't feel ready for. "I wish you were going to be with me. You could be on the track team, and we could have lunch together . . ."

"*I* wish you could do school with me."

"Me too." Arden got to pick all her own homeschool projects, and as long as she got her work done it didn't matter if she finished up by lunchtime and could spend the rest of the day doing whatever she wanted. Last year, her mama had let her spend a whole school year studying the changes in the water plants by the bay's edge and called it botany, while my science class had to dissect frogs. I'd smelled like formaldehyde for days.

"Mom's already planning a whole unit on aeronautics. We're going to take a day trip to Kitty Hawk and everything. Mom says maybe if the weather's nice we'll rent a condo on the beach for a few days, maybe drive up to Corolla and see the wild horses."

"It sounds nice." I squeezed the paintbrush in my hand. What would *my* family be doing this autumn?

Would Mama be in the hospital by the time I got back to school at the end of August?

"Want to go for a run with me tomorrow?" Arden asked.

"No." I liked swimming, and when school was in session I did fine in PE, but as far as I was concerned, running was *not* something a person should do for fun, especially when it was hitting triple-digit temperatures before breakfast.

"Is . . . something going on with you, Della?" Arden asked, dipping her brush back into the Styrofoam plate we'd filled with paint. She kept her eyes on the plywood wall as she drew her brush across it, leaving a thick green streak in its wake. She was watching that wall so hard she might have been waiting for it to sprout flowers or start talking.

"I'm fine." All week long, the words I'd wanted to say

had fizzled before they hit my tongue, leaving me with a whole lot of buzzing in my head and no way to let it out. I'd wanted more than anything to talk to Arden about my mama and the things that had started coming out of her mouth again, but every time I'd been with her, I found I just couldn't. There was always something else going on: her brother and sisters causing trouble, or customers coming to the farm stand just as I opened my mouth to spill out the truth, or a little spark of worry in her eyes that made my skin crawl uneasily.

What could Arden do, anyway? The Hawthornes and the Kellys were twined together like the branches of a weeping willow, but in the twelve years since Mama's sickness came on, the best they'd been able to do was watch me when things got extra bad four years ago.

Arden painted right over the same spot she'd just done, like she didn't even notice it. She looked hurt, her eyebrows pinched together just a tiny bit in the middle, her cheek pulled in like she was chewing on it.

"You sure? You've just been so quiet. You didn't even laugh when I asked you to go for a run. Is . . . is something the matter with your mama?"

"She's fine." A trio of ladybugs flew around our heads, their pointed red wings blurring with their flight. One after another, they came to rest on the top of the playhouse. In the sunshine, they looked like little jewels, shining and bright and such a rich scarlet color my eyes could hardly take it in.

Four years ago, when Mama's sickness had gotten so bad, the doctor had taken her away and put her in the mental hospital in Alberta. I couldn't see her for weeks and weeks; I'd had to stay with Arden's family every time Daddy drove out to visit. I could still remember crawling into Daddy's bed every night after I was supposed to have already been asleep, asking him if Mama was ever gonna come back to us.

I'd opened that Emily Dickinson book from Miss Lorena's box library yesterday, let the pages fall open in the middle until my heart was full up with the smell of old books. Most of the poems in it I didn't much understand, but I liked the way they sounded, the way they pulled at something inside of me. There had been one that talked about grief, about how sometimes it hurts to live.

That's how it had felt when Mama went away to the Alberta hospital last time.

If I told Arden about the things that had been happening this week, it would make it real—make it so I couldn't ignore or explain away the things Mama had said, the way she'd been so much worse than she ever had been since the bad time after Grandpa Case died.

"Rena!" Arden shouted, so loud I almost let my paintbrush tumble into the dirt. "Put that snake back where you got it, and leave Charlotte alone."

Rena looked up at us so fast her hair bounced, and then dropped the garter snake she'd been teasing her little sister with, so it could slither back away into the marsh.

Arden looked back at me. "You sure, Dell?"

"Positive," I said, hoping it was true, knowing I had to find a way to fix Mama for good before she disappeared like that again. Last night, hearing Mama talk about Grandpa Case like he was still alive and talking to her, that had been bad. But it couldn't be too late yet—it just couldn't.

I'd been littler the last time Mama had gotten so sick. I hadn't been able to help as much. Maybe this time, *I* could make the difference.

CHAPTER EIGHT

That Saturday morning when I went out to do my chores it had already hit a hundred degrees even though it wasn't eight o'clock yet, and big fat droplets of sweat rolled off me as I searched through the straw in the henhouse looking for eggs. Our best layer, Matilda, liked to hide them in new places every time, and more than once I'd missed some only to smash them flat by accident later on. Daddy was already out in the fields, trying to fix one of his irrigation sprinklers where it had stopped spraying right; he'd been awake and gone before I'd even gotten out of bed.

I'd snuck the Emily Dickinson book out with me, and after I'd finished collecting the eggs into my basket,

I sat down beside the coop and let the pages flutter open. They landed on a poem called "Book":

There is no Frigate like a Book
To take us Lands away
Nor any Coursers like a Page
Of prancing Poetry—

I smiled. I didn't know what frigates or coursers were, but somehow in this hot and awful week, Miss Emily's book was just the thing that helped me fly away from the drought and the way the heat made me feel more dead than alive. The precise march of those words in the little blue book was like an equation, the way they all knew just where they belonged in the poem.

I'd just closed the book when Arden came into view from around the house, her face flushed red with the heat, her light brown hair in a pair of French braids already starting to come loose and frizzy at the edges.

"Mom sent me over to see if I could borrow some eggs," she said as soon as she saw me. "About a million things are up with our hens and they didn't give any this morning."

"Sure. We've got plenty." I stood up. "Come inside and I'll see if we've got a carton you can borrow."

The house fans were working overtime, all of them going so hard that the whole house sounded like it was pulsing. They were loud enough that it wasn't till I got all the way in the door, Arden so close behind me I could feel her breath on my back, that I realized that Mylie was screaming in our bedroom—the kind of ear-bleeding scream that meant she was either hurt or really, *really* mad. Even with all the fits she'd been throwing lately, I hadn't heard her screaming like this since she fell off the front porch and dislocated her elbow right at the beginning of spring.

Mama was perched like a bird on the edge of the couch in the living room, twisting her hands the same way she'd been doing when we watched the detective show on Thursday night. She'd chewed her bottom lip so hard it had turned red, the blood welling up bright and angry where her teeth had pulled off all the skin.

"Mama?" I asked, coming inside and setting my basket down on the floor. Arden stayed behind me, stuck in the doorway, so still she was hardly breathing. I stepped forward and snapped my fingers right in front of Mama's face. "Mama! You gonna go get Mylie out of her crib?"

From the bedroom, Mylie's screaming ratcheted up another few degrees. Mama didn't answer. "Did Mylie get in trouble?" I asked. "You gonna be mad if I get her up? She sounds real upset, Mama."

Mama still didn't say anything, just looked at me with a little dip in her forehead and that red, red blood on her lip. I stared at her, feeling the sweat trickling ticklishly down my neck and into my collar.

"Mama?" I whispered, praying as hard as I'd ever prayed in my life that she'd wake up and pay attention to me. "Mama, you gonna go get Mylie up or should I?"

"Leave me be, Della," Mama said, flexing her fingers out and then curling them back up again, her hands white as flour. "It's safer for her. Too many bad things can happen to a little baby."

There were tears shining bright in Mama's eyes. "My poor baby. I gotta keep her safe, Della. I got to do what's best for her."

Her face was all twisted, like there was a war going on inside her mind between her regular self and the voice that told her that Mylie wasn't safe. My skin went all fluttery, and it took everything I had not to yell or cry like a baby myself. I wished Daddy would come in, or that I even knew where he was to go find him, but he could be out there anywhere on the tractor and I'd never be able to run across two hundred acres of land to hunt him down.

I was all the help I was going to get.

I turned back to Arden. Her chocolate-brown eyes were big and round, her lips so pale she looked half sick herself.

"Do you . . . need any help?"

I shook my head. Letting Arden in there seemed almost worse than going in there myself.

"Don't worry about the eggs," Arden said, already stepping backward down the steps into the yard.

"Wait," I said, darting a glance behind me at Mama and then lowering my voice to a whisper. My whole body buzzed with urgency, like I'd burn up with the crops out in the field if I couldn't make Arden understand me. "Listen. Don't tell your parents about this, okay? Don't tell *anyone*."

Arden went even paler, her face almost green. "But—"

"*No*," I hissed, "you have to promise me, okay? Not *anyone*."

Arden hesitated for a long minute, but then nodded.

"I'll explain later. Another day," I said, and let the screen door slam shut as Arden turned and ran back toward her own house.

I was still holding the Emily Dickinson book. My stomach roiled and rocked with a sick kind of guilt—if I'd just come in sooner, if I hadn't snuck that little blue book outside and dawdled while I was doing my chores, could I have stopped things before they got this bad?

"Okay, Mama. I'm just gonna go get Mylie up now, right?" In the bedroom Mylie's screaming had started hitching, like she was hiccuping so hard she couldn't even cry properly anymore. I kind of thought I knew how she felt.

As soon as I opened my bedroom door the smell hit me, so bad I had to put my hand up over my nose as I walked over to the crib. Mylie's pajama shorts were wet through, her diaper hanging so low off her bum it might as well not even be there, and there was a smear of brown on her leg.

"You have gotta be kidding me," I said, opening up the wipe box and pulling out as many as I could hold. "Sorry, Mylie baby, I just gotta clean you up before I can get you out of there." I wiped all over her legs and back. Mylie had stopped screaming but the hiccups were still coming, her whole body shuddering hard from all that crying. "Sorry, sweetheart." I tried not to gag on the stinky-diaper smell. "You're really messy this morning." How long had Mama left her in here crying? Mylie had still been sleeping when I'd woken up and gone out to get the eggs, but from how upset she was, I guessed she'd been crying the whole time since.

When I'd got up as much of the mess as I could

without taking her diaper off, I picked Mylie up under the arms and carried her over to the changing table, not letting her wet shorts touch any part of me. I pulled off her pajamas and changed her diaper as fast as I could, then dropped that mess of a diaper in the pail and picked Mylie up for real this time, wrapping my arms around her and hugging her as tight as I could. She was getting pretty big now, but still felt so little and sad, whimpering and shaking like she couldn't remember how to be happy anymore.

"Shh," I whispered, bouncing up and down on my heels a little like Mama used to do when Mylie was colicky as a newborn. "Hey, sweet baby, you're gonna be just fine, I promise. I got you now. I got you."

Slowly, Mylie's shudders slowed down and her whimpering quieted. She reached up and put her arms around my neck, her hands and face all wet and goobery from sweat and tears and snot.

"You're okay," I said, rubbing her back with one of my hands. Her skin was still smooth as a newborn baby's, softer than the down on a peach just off the tree.

"Stowy?" Mylie asked, her little voice wobbling.

I bit my lip, thinking of Miss Tabitha at church last week. If Daddy hadn't been standing right there, would I have asked her?

"Stowy?"

"Sure, Mylie baby." I set her back down on the changing table and found a watermelon-print sundress—one that had been mine when I was a baby. I pulled it over her head. "You know the O'Connells down south of Arden's folks? This story's about them. When Mrs. O'Connell was a little girl, her daddy died, and her whole heart filled up with black sadness, so much that it leaked out and made a dark cloud that followed her everywhere she went. Nothing anyone did could dissolve that black cloud—until her mama finally took her to the Quigleys."

Mylie was quiet now, sitting still while I buttoned up her dress and used a wipe to clean all the mess off her face.

"The Bee Lady had a cup of tea made up before the O'Connells had even got inside the house, all sweetened up with a bright glittering gold honey that looked like yellow diamonds. As soon as Mrs. O'Connell took the first sip of that tea, the storm cloud she carried with her started to break up—and when she'd drained the cup dry, the sun was shining out of her brighter than out of the sky itself."

"Wan' Mama," Mylie said after I'd finished the story.

Thinking of Mama brought that fluttery feeling back

to my skin, and my hands started shaking, just a little bit, as I tossed the wipe I'd used on Mylie's face into the garbage. This morning had been even worse than last week and the watermelon seeds. My mind kept replaying it over and over like it was a movie—Mama leaving Mylie to scream and scream and scream in her crib, telling me it was safer for her. *Safer.* How could Mama think that?

My hands shook even harder. "Dell?" Mylie asked, peering up at my face, her chin quivering like she was thinking about crying again.

I took a deep breath. "It's all right, Mylie baby," I said, trying to make my voice as calm as a mama on TV. "Guess I just need some breakfast, and you do, too."

But it was more than being hungry that was causing those shakes, I knew. It was Mama. It was Mama, seeming deeper in her sickness than she had been for years.

Mama and Daddy met when they were both at college in Greenville, back when cell phones didn't do email. Mama always said they fell for each other so fast and hard that they just knew they wanted a family together, so they had me.

Except right after I was born, things started going wrong with Mama. She'd hear people talking to her who weren't there, or forget things that were pretty important, or not know to be sad at sad things and happy at happy ones. Eventually, she went to see a doctor and he told her she had a brain disease with a long name I can't spell: schizophrenia. The doctor had said it came on because of a "hormonal trigger," that somehow my birth had been the thing that tipped her into the sickness. He said she also had some other problems that made her always so anxious about germs and stuff.

That Greenville doctor gave her some medicines to try, and although one of them made her face twitchy and she sometimes still heard strange voices or mixed up sad and happy, she did okay until I was eight years old and her daddy—my grandpa Case—died. I'd always thought he was pretty old, but Mama said he was still young for a grandpa, and nobody expected him to have a heart attack. Nobody thought the doctors wouldn't be able to fix his heart, either, but when they couldn't, it hit Mama hard.

It hit all of us hard, but especially Mama.

I squeezed my eyes shut, holding on to Mylie and being glad she hadn't been around back then. Mama had gotten real, real sick, till things got so bad she didn't know who any of us were anymore and couldn't tell things that were true from things that were only in her head. One day she'd taken too many pills, and Daddy had called Dr. DuBose, and Dr. DuBose had told Daddy he needed to get Mama to the hospital fast.

She didn't come back for more than a month.

After that things got better, because Dr. DuBose had found a different medication that worked better than anything the first doctor had tried, a medication that helped Mama's brain make sense of things the way they were. And for a long time everything had been great— almost like having a regular, healthy mama who never had to worry about spending months in the hospital or losing track of what was real and what wasn't. The new medicine sometimes made her forget things, and every now and then she complained that it made her brain feel like it wasn't as smart as it used to be.

But for a long while, things were good.

Until Mama had Mylie, and she started getting worse again. It had been slow at first, just little things that didn't matter so much. Like how Mama hadn't let Daddy get the air-conditioning fixed when it broke, or the way she'd sometimes have a hard time getting out of bed. *Be patient*, Daddy had told me every time I'd brought it up.

"It's just like after you were born, Della," he'd said. "Having a baby is hard on any woman, and even harder on somebody with your mama's illness. We just have to hold on till things regulate in her body, honey. Your mama's had this sickness a long time, and you and me and her, we've been through a lot together. We can get through this, too. It's just going to take a little patience."

But this wasn't little. And I had a feeling it was going to take more than just patience to solve it.

Above my head the ceiling fan pumped and pumped, but it was still so hot in that room that it made my head feel dizzy and weak. I scooped Mylie up off the changing table and hugged her one more time.

"It's okay, Mylie baby," I whispered, giving her a big kiss on her soft little cheek. "It's gonna be just fine. It's not gonna be like it was last time, okay? I'll make sure it isn't."

I took a deep breath, trying to fill up every inch of my lungs, feeling the humidity hanging in the air like it wanted to rain so bad but couldn't. "I know something that can fix her. I've got a plan."

"Pwan?" Mylie asked.

"Yes, you silly little parrot. I know you don't even know what a *plan* is, but I've got one. Remember Grandpa's leg," I whispered to Mylie, hugging her tight. "Remember Mrs. O'Connell's black cloud and all the other Bee Stories. I'll talk to Miss Tabitha tomorrow at church. And then, Mylie, absolutely *everything* is going to be okay."

It *would* be okay. It would have to be.

Because if Miss Tabitha's honey didn't heal Mama, I didn't know if anything could.

CHAPTER NINE

Mama managed to get through the rest of Saturday—and the church service the next day—without saying anything too outlandish, even if she did seem quieter than normal, her face twisting itself into pinched-looking grimaces every now and again. I wasn't sure if Daddy was pretending not to notice or really so distracted he didn't see any of it, but either way, he didn't say a thing about it to Mama or me.

We were all on our way out to the car after church when I caught sight of Miss Tabitha leaving the sanctuary.

"I gotta run to the bathroom," I said, stopping as the rest of my family went through the doors to the outside.

"Can't it wait till we get home?" Daddy asked, rubbing at his forehead.

"Uh-uh. I'll be quick."

Daddy sighed and waved me off toward the bathroom. I waited until the doors had closed behind them, and then stood up as straight as I could and marched up to Miss Tabitha, where she was standing talking to Mr. Anton Jones, jingling a little silver bell bracelet on her freckled white wrist every now and again. I hung back until Mr. Anton had nodded politely at Miss Tabitha and gone on out to the parking lot.

Before I could even open my mouth to say anything at all, Miss Tabitha turned to me, blue eyes bright.

"Why, Della Kelly," she said. "It's good to see you, shug. You need something?"

I nodded, but no matter how hard I tried, the words wouldn't seem to come to my tongue. I thought of another Bee Story, this one about Miss Tabitha herself: how a few years back Wanda Ann Rosemond's fiancé had jilted her right at the altar in this very church, and it had broke Wanda Ann's heart into so many pieces that she couldn't stop crying no matter how hard she tried.

Pretty soon she'd cried so many tears that she'd made her own little rainstorm, following her everywhere she went, weeping salty drops onto anyone who stood too close to her. She'd gone to Miss Tabitha for some honey, and just one taste had dried up everything around her and pulled those pieces of her heart back together, to boot.

Miss Tabitha was still looking at me, her eyebrows floating up just a bit.

"It's my mama," I said, the words so quiet she had to lean in closer to hear me. "She—well—"

"Yes?"

"Your honey." Now I was whispering. "Have you got anything that might—"

"It isn't a cold your mama's had, is it?" the Bee Lady asked, her own voice nearly as quiet as mine. I shook my head. "I didn't think so. But I won't say anything about it, not if you and your daddy aren't ready to talk yet."

I wondered how many secrets the Bee Lady had locked up in her head—all those secrets of all those people who had come to her, for longer than I'd been alive, asking for her honey to be a little miracle they could take the lid off and hold in their hands.

"So do you? Have you got anything that might be able to . . . fix her?"

Miss Tabitha shook her head right away, and something in me twirled its way down to my toes. "No, ma'am. I'm sorry, Della. Nothing I've got can do more than her doctor's already doing. She's under the best care, shug. She's got a good doctor, and she's on the right medications."

"But those pills aren't enough! She needs something better. Something *permanent*. She didn't even have schizophrenia till I was born, Miss Tabitha! If she didn't always have it, surely that means there's something out there that could make her *stop* having it."

"Far as I know, there isn't anything out there that can heal a person of what your mama's got, not when the good Lord saw fit to make her that way." Miss Tabitha's eyes were so kind it hurt to look at them.

"But there has to be *something*! Your honey, it can do anything! It fixed Grandpa's leg by the time the sun set that day—it healed Mrs. O'Connell's black cloud of sadness—it patched up Wanda Ann's heart so she wasn't bringing the rain down anymore!"

There was more, too, more Bee Stories—like the little jar of creamy white honey that Miss Tabitha had given Mama a few months ago to help Mylie sleep better at night, or the way the Packards swore Miss Tabitha's honey had healed their two-year-old's pneumonia the moment the honey had touched baby George's lips. Those Bee Stories felt like a part of me, a part of Maryville itself, woven into the history of every family in town.

But my tongue was frozen again, stuck inside my mouth like it had been glued there.

"I'm sorry, Della," Miss Tabitha said again, and I could hear the regret threaded all the way through her voice like little dusts of pollen in golden honey, but it still didn't stop the anger that was rising up in me.

"I don't have anything that can heal your mama," Miss Tabitha went on, her voice gentle and low. "But I've got something that could heal *you*, if you wanted."

"Isn't anything wrong with me," I said, mad that she'd got my hopes up in the first place, even though she hadn't said anything to me but to ask if I needed anything. People talked such great things about the Bee Lady, and yet here she was—not even able to figure out that it was Mama who needed fixing, not me.

"Still," Miss Tabitha said. "You just let me know, Della. You just let me know."

I was quiet all through the ride home, leaning my head up against the window of the truck and feeling the engine's rumble all the way through to my clenched-together teeth.

There had to be a way to fix Mama, just *had* to be, no matter what Mama's doctors said. Strong fingers reached in and squeezed at my heart until I could hardly breathe.

I'd been the one who had made Mama the way she was.

And I needed to be the one to fix it.

The new plan came to me that night. As I tossed and turned in my bed, playing back over the conversation with the Bee Lady and getting madder and madder every minute, something that Dr. DuBose had said last time Mama had been in the hospital came into my mind.

I'd been eight years old and in the hospital waiting room, not allowed to see Mama because I was too young, crying and angry and not old enough to even understand exactly what was going on. Dr. DuBose had come to sit down beside me, his mustache twitching as he'd smiled and put a gentle hand on mine.

"I know this is hard, Della," he'd said, his voice deep and slow. "I know you miss your mama, and we're working hard to get her back to you as soon as we can. But it's best for her to be here for a while. Her brain needs a rest, so it can get better the way it needs to."

Lying there in my bed, those remembered words slipped right into and through me. I'd only been eight then, but now I was twelve and could do lots more. *I* could help Mama's brain get a rest. I'd do so much to help her around the house that she wouldn't have to do anything at all, and with all that resting, her brain was bound to heal. And not just a temporary fix, like the few years of right thinking she'd gotten from her new medication. *Real* healing. Permanently. Fixed so perfectly that by the time Mylie and I were grown up, we'd all laugh to think that Mama had once had such trouble.

I thought about what Arden had seen the day before, and hoped just about as hard as I ever had that she'd made good on her promise and not said anything to her parents. I'd told Mama and Daddy I had a stomachache and begged out of going to my usual shift at the farm stand, and Miss Amanda had had to send Eli to stay with Arden instead. It had made *all* the grown-ups cranky, but I hadn't been able to face Arden yet. I knew exactly how her eyes would've followed me, glaring until I'd spilled the whole truth. But now, maybe I could get Mama heading toward healthy before Arden—or anyone else—had time to do much worrying at all.

I settled deeper into my pillows and closed my eyes. Tomorrow.

Tomorrow was going to be the start of something a whole lot better.

CHAPTER TEN

Mama had Mylie up and dressed by the time I'd finished gathering the eggs the next day, and Mylie was sitting in her high chair drinking juice with a big smile on her face while Mama penciled in the crossword.

She was always good at the crosswords—words, Mama had said to me ever since I could remember, were her best thing. They sure weren't mine, though; I'd always done better with numbers, which never go and change on you when you aren't expecting it. You couldn't grow up with a mama like mine and not get to liking reading, but I still had a hard time in English class, especially if we were supposed to read something aloud to the whole room, which was a surefire way to make me blush all the way to the roots of my hair.

The place where I *was* good with my words was telling stories to people I knew well: Mylie, or Mama and Daddy, or Arden. I liked the feeling of those stories rising up inside me, filling me with light and wonder. Math made me feel close to Daddy, but stories made me feel close to Mama. She had been telling me stories as long as I could remember—fairy tales, Bee Stories, funny things about what she got up to when she was growing up. One year, when I was five or six, I'd had trouble falling asleep at nights, and Mama had sat by my bed and told me stories about a family of kittens who got up to mischief until I'd drifted off to sleep.

Sometimes, even now, I could still hear her soft voice telling those kitten stories when I closed my eyes at bedtime.

"Got a bunch of eggs this morning," I said, sailing past the table to the stove and pulling out a frying pan. Cooking wasn't really my best thing, either, but I knew that if I was going to carry through on my plan to fix Mama's brain, I needed to practice. I turned the heat up under the pan halfway, just like Mama always did, and put a dollop of butter inside it.

"You find Matilda's?" Mama asked me without looking up.

"Cluck! Cluck!" shouted Mylie, banging her cup on

the high-chair tray. Mama reached over, eyes still on the crossword, and pushed Mylie's cup down so she couldn't bang it again.

"Mm-hmm." The butter was starting to melt and sizzle against the pan now, filling the kitchen up with that sharp warm smell butter gets when it's cooking. I wiped sweat off my forehead with the back of my hand and cracked six eggs into the pan as carefully as possible, but a few shell pieces still snuck in. I tried to grab them out with my finger, hoping hard that Mama wouldn't look up and yell at me for having my hands in the food, which was the thing she hated more than just about anything in the world.

Good thing the crossword was keeping her pretty busy.

"There," said Mama a minute later, after I'd finished fishing out the eggshells and grabbed a rubber spatula to scramble up the eggs. "I got every single one. Ha! Your mama's vocabulary is as extensive as it is erudite, Della."

She looked up at me, her smile freezing as she noticed the pan I was stirring. "You know I don't like you to turn on the stove without asking, hon. What are you doing?"

"Just making some breakfast," I said, leaving the eggs for a minute to wash a couple of peaches. "So you don't have to."

"Goodness, what's come over you?" Mama asked, but there was a laugh in her voice, and I knew she wasn't mad. I breathed a teeny little sigh of relief. "Usually it feels like pulling teeth to get you to do chores around here."

I bit the inside of my cheek, knowing Mama was right and feeling about as bad as I could feel. Was that part of the reason she was getting sick again?

"Better turn that off," Mama said. "Smells like it's burning." I jumped and looked back at the pan, which was starting to smoke just a little. I pulled it off the heat and stirred the eggs up again, frowning at the little brown bits and the way a layer of egg was stuck tight to the bottom of the skillet. It was going to take a lot of scrubbing to get it clean, but I hoped it would be worth it.

I popped four slices of bread into the toaster and started cutting up the peaches, pulling the little paring knife around the peach pits slowly and carefully, just like Mama had shown me when I was younger.

"I'm going to help you extra from now on, Mama, I promise," I said, arranging the peach slices on a plate and spreading butter and strawberry jam on the toast. "That way you can get plenty of rest."

"Rest?" Mama said, a funny look on her face, but before she could say anything else, the back door banged open and Daddy came inside.

"I think it's gonna be even hotter than yesterday," Daddy said, wiping his face with his shoulder and leaving a big dark sweaty mark on his sleeve. He came into the kitchen and ran his hands under the cold water for a long, long minute, cooling himself down just as much as he was washing up. "It keeps on like this, eastern North Carolina will end up looking like Death Valley before long."

Mama patted the chair next to her. "Come on and sit down, Miles. Della made us breakfast."

"Thought I smelled something funny," Daddy said, but he winked at me. I balanced the toast plate in one hand and the peach plate in the other and brought them to the table, then grabbed the pan of eggs and added that, too. I gave Mylie a piece of toast, which she promptly dumped upside down on her tray and rubbed around.

"Wed!" she shouted, pointing at the red jam smeared across her tray. "Woooooah." She cackled and swooped her fat white fingers through the jam like it was finger paint.

Mama didn't say anything, just put a peach slice on Mylie's high-chair tray, so that I wondered if she even saw or heard anything else going on in the kitchen. Her face was pulled into a strange shape, a sour, wrong-looking kind of grimace, like she was in pain. I turned away quick, my hand tight around my fork. I wished for the hundredth time that my conversation with Miss Tabitha yesterday had gone differently. How could she not *see* how important this was?

"I'm still worried about my watermelons," Daddy told Mama as he dished eggs onto his plate. "Ben thinks maybe it's anthracnose fungus. Gave me some kind of oil to try, but if it doesn't work, I might have to give up on keeping them organic this year and order some of the stuff my daddy always used. I'm starting to wonder if I was wrong to try to make so many changes at once after my daddy had to leave last year, Suzanne. We just can't afford to lose this batch of melons right now."

Daddy sighed. Way back when he'd gone to college he'd studied agriculture science. He and Grandpa had always had different ideas about how to run things on the farm—Grandpa wanted to do it the way his daddy and his granddaddy had done it, while Daddy wanted to try some of the things he'd learned in college, things Grandpa scoffed at and called ridiculous. Like getting rid of all the chemicals Grandpa had used, and putting the big spiral tiller in the shed and investing in other equipment Daddy said wouldn't hurt the soil as much.

"I'll keep my fingers crossed for Ben's oil," Mama

said, like she'd come back to earth again from wherever she'd been a minute ago.

I tried to eat my breakfast as fast as Daddy did, and by the time he'd got up from the table and headed back outside, I was already gathering up plates from the table and rinsing them in the sink so they could go right into the dishwasher.

"I like this new version of you, Della," said Mama, heading toward the sink, where Mylie's washcloth was drying over the faucet.

"Let me wipe Mylie up," I said, grabbing the washcloth before Mama could and getting it wet.

Mylie squirmed away, squealing, "No way!" as I tried to wipe her, but I made growling noises and chased her with the washcloth till she giggled and opened her fingers for me to clean. She was a mess, strings of peach flesh wrapped around her fingers and bright red jam smeared all over her cheeks and stuffed up her nose.

"I'm gonna take care of Mylie for you today, Mama," I said, pulling out the high-chair tray and picking Mylie up. "That way you can rest, all right?"

Mama put her hands on her hips. "I appreciate the thought, Della honey, but I don't need any rest, and I'm not sure where you came by the idea that I do. It's my job to keep you and Mylie safe. Besides, you gotta go help your daddy this morning and then watch the farm stand—you know full well Arden can't stay there all by herself. Who knows what might happen to her all alone on that highway?"

I stood planted there in the middle of the kitchen, Mylie hot and sweaty in my arms, little drafts of breeze trickling down from the ceiling fan. "You sure?" I said finally, hugging Mylie a little tighter and feeling old and young, all at the same time.

Mama nodded, her face relaxing and softening, the way the sky unwrinkles after a thunderstorm. "Of course."

"If you're *really* sure," I said, remembering all the ways Mama hadn't been her normal self lately. Mama nodded one more time, and I sighed and handed Mylie over to her. Mama's arm was slick with sweat where it brushed against mine, and her red cheeks made her look as hot as I felt. For just a minute I found myself thinking about rain, about the way most Carolina summers brought thunderstorms nearly every afternoon, pounding the houses and the dirt and your skin with so much water all at once that it ran like a river through the gutters and irrigation canals.

Right then, I don't know if Daddy or I was wishing harder for one of those big, beautiful rainstorms.

CHAPTER ELEVEN

Daddy was working on butter beans when I got outside, tossing the picked pods into a bucket with a quick *snap-snap-snap*. Without looking up at me, he pointed down the row a ways, to a section he hadn't reached yet, and I dropped down into a squat and started feeling through the bean plants for the fat green pods, the ones that were just ripe enough but not so old their beans had already lost that buttery softness. A box of fresh-picked butter beans would hardly last a day out at the stand, they were that good.

Neither of us talked. Me and Daddy had always had something special—sometimes, before Mylie came along and Grandma and Grandpa Kelly moved to

Alberta, before the worry wrinkles took up permanent residence on Daddy's face, the two of us would sit on the back porch step and look out over the farm fields, and he'd put his arm around my shoulder and squeeze and call me his best little girl. We used to sit there while he helped me with my homework, or quizzed me on interesting math problems he knew I'd like, or told dumb math jokes that made us both laugh till we nearly cried.

But all year he'd been quieter than usual, constantly rubbing his forehead like he does when he's tired and walking around like he carried a fifty-pound bag of Kelly Family Farm wheat over each shoulder.

"Daddy, here's some advice," I said, forcing my voice to sound cheerful. "At a job interview, always tell them you're ready to give a hundred and ten percent." I paused for effect. "Except if that job's for a statistician."

Daddy grunted but didn't even look up. I shrugged away the tickle of a drop of sweat making its way between my shoulder blades.

There wasn't anything I could do to take away Daddy's stress about the farm, but maybe I *could* at least help him feel easier about Mama.

I scooted down the row, pulling my bucket of bean pods after me, my thoughts twisting around all the ways I could help Mama out this summer so she could rest more. The closest grocery store was more than halfway to Alberta, so she'd have to drive us, but what if I told her she could sit in the car and read while I took Mylie into the store and bought the groceries?

I could do more cleaning around the house, too, but I had a feeling that if I tried that, Mama would just follow right along after me, doing things the "right" way. There was a reason most of my chores were outside—Mama was awfully particular about cleaning. It was okay if I loaded up the dishwasher, or cooked a little as long as I was extra careful to have clean hands and never touch the food I was cooking, but things like scrubbing counters and toilets and windows were Mama's special responsibility. Daddy told me once, a long time ago, that it was part of Mama's sickness; that making sure everything was sparkling clean was the one thing she could do to feel a little in control when everything inside her was going wrong.

I took a deep breath and stood up, stretching out my legs, which were sore from all that squatting. Daddy and I had picked the whole row of butter beans clean without saying hardly anything to each other. The silence was thick and heavy all around us, like the heat and humidity that pressed into my skin until all I wanted to do was stick my whole self in the refrigerator to get some relief.

"Think that's it for this morning," Daddy said, picking up both our buckets in the same great big hand. "Nothin' else ripe enough to harvest again just yet. There ought to be a crop of watermelon, but all the ripe ones have come down with disease this week."

His face was gleaming with sweat and there was a streak of dirt across his forehead, where he'd rubbed it with his fingers. "You want a ride over to the stand on the tractor, Dell?"

"Sure," I said. There were only a few acres between the farm garden and the highway, but any walking in this heat sent dizzy swoopings through my head. I followed Daddy to where the John Deere was parked, its green paint turned yellow from all the dust and pollen caked onto it. I climbed up behind him and held on around his waist, trying to ignore the fact that even through his T-shirt I could feel how sweaty he was.

Then again, he was probably thinking the same thing about me.

We were nearly out to the road when a blue sedan pulled into our driveway. Thomas had come out to help a couple times already, usually staying far out on the farm with Daddy, but every now and then coming up to the kitchen for a glass of icy tea sweetened with Quigley honey, or a plate of cold watermelon. He was easy to talk to, even for me—and despite the fact that he was getting ready to start his last year of high school, he treated me like an adult.

Just as the engine on the Bradleys' car turned off, the tractor gave a shuddering thump and stopped dead in the driveway. Daddy banged his fist down on the steering wheel and swore so loud and dirty it made me jump. I'd never heard Daddy use so many bad words all in a row, and almost never heard him yell like that. I swallowed, feeling that sandpapery sensation of a dry throat on a hot day, and hopped down as quick as I could.

Daddy followed me, pacing around to the front of the John Deere and throwing up the hood. He said another dirty word and brought his fingers up to rub at his forehead, leaving a smear of grease across his skin to match the smudge of dirt there.

Thomas got out of the car and called over to us. "Everything okay, Mr. Kelly?"

"Not really," said Daddy, his face tight and stretched like he was having to work every second to keep his anger in. "Know anything about fixing tractors?"

Thomas laughed incredulously. "You know I'm a city boy, Mr. Kelly. I wouldn't know a tractor if it bit me. Didn't even need a riding mower at my old place."

Daddy sighed, kicking at one of the tractor wheels.

"Knew I should've gone ahead and replaced the belt when Anton said to. This is the last thing I need right now. You go on to the stand with Arden, Della. I've gotta go back to the house and call Anton to ask him to order the part I need."

"You sure?" I asked, watching Arden wave at me out of the corner of my eye. After I'd skipped out of my shift at the farm stand Saturday, Arden had tried to call twice yesterday afternoon, but I'd made sure I wasn't around when the phone got picked up. I didn't want to hear what she had to say about the things she'd seen Saturday morning, after Mama had left Mylie to cry in her crib. I didn't want Arden doing her best to convince me my plans weren't going to work out.

Daddy tried to smile, a sad little thing that only made it halfway up his mouth. "This tractor won't be going anywhere under its own steam till it's got a new belt," he said, taking a big deep breath and raking his hands through his hair. "You go on with Arden. I'll go tell your mama what happened."

He turned and started walking down the driveway to where Thomas waited, but I stayed there by the tractor for just a minute, watching him go. Before, while we were picking the butter beans, he'd looked weighed down by a hundred pounds of his own wheat, his shoulders hunched and his head heavy.

Now he looked like he was carrying all the wheat in the world.

I stopped by the mailbox at the end of our drive on my way to the farm stand, more out of habit than anything else, but smiled when I saw that the only thing in there was a little pink postcard from Grandma Kelly.

Dear watermelon girl, it said in Grandma's old-fashioned loopy writing. *Hope you're not forgetting us out there on that farm. Come visit soon. XOXO.* I tucked it into the pocket of my shorts, wishing Grandma was there right that moment to give me one of her grandma hugs. We could *all* use a good grandma hug about now, I reckoned. Even though Alberta was only an hour away, it felt like we hardly saw Grandma and Grandpa anymore, with Daddy so busy all the time and Mama trying to keep up with Mylie's mischief.

Arden's face was pinched and worried looking when I made it to the stand. Before I could even flop down into the empty camp chair, she'd pounced.

"You tell me this instant what's going on, Della Kelly. I've been worried sick about you all weekend. How come you didn't answer any of my calls?"

I didn't answer, just grabbed a Dixie cup and filled

it up with water from the ice-cold cooler sitting on the table.

"*Della*. Come on."

I sighed and sat down, holding my cup so tight in my hands that the paper sides squeezed together and some of the water sloshed onto my palms.

"I think my mama's getting sick again." I felt heavier than ever, like saying it out loud had made it somehow more real than before. I swallowed hard and looked out across the highway, heat rising up from the pavement and creeping its way under the awning to wrap us up in its arms. "*Really* sick. Like—like a long time ago." I knew that Arden remembered the bad time just as well as I did.

"Oh, Della, really?"

"It's been bad. But you can't tell anyone at all. You have to swear to me. I don't want anybody sending Mama back to the hospital."

I stuck my pinkie out, waiting for her promise.

Arden's forehead scrunched up. "Are you sure, Della? If she's getting bad like last time, maybe your daddy needs to take her to the doctor."

"He tried. She won't go."

"Well then . . . maybe—maybe the hospital is where she needs to be, for a while, if she's that sick."

"No. Don't tell *anyone*." I scraped at the dirt under my fingernails. "She needs more than that this time. More than just a Band-Aid. She needs something different, something that can heal her all the way, forever."

"Is that possible?"

"It *has* to be. Don't you get that? If it were your mama, you'd feel the same way. I *have* to find a way to fix her. I have to. Just promise me you won't tell anybody."

Arden sighed, but nodded, and joined her pinkie with mine. "I guess so," she said, but the worry stayed right there between her eyebrows. For one wild moment, I thought about taking it all back, thought about going and knocking on Miss Amanda's door and telling her what was going on with Mama myself.

But I didn't. Miss Amanda and Mr. Ben were nice. Nicer than nice. They were practically my other parents. And they'd helped us plenty when Mama went to the hospital. But even then, all they'd been able to do was to mind me when Daddy had to go visit Mama. There wasn't anything more they could do now, except maybe pester Mama about going to those doctor's visits she kept skipping, and stress her out even more so she got worse faster. Plus, Miss Amanda and Mr. Ben had plenty of other things to take care of: their own kids, their own farm.

And Daddy—he was worried just like I was, I knew. But he had other worries than just Mama, with the farm, and now the tractor breaking, and all his watermelon plants coming down with disease.

The one person who needed Mama healed more than anybody, the one person who couldn't bear the idea of turning thirteen next year and becoming a teenager without a healthy mama to guide her, the one person who didn't have anybody else to worry about—that was me. It was up to me now.

It was all up to me.

CHAPTER TWELVE

Summer evenings in Maryville are just about as hot as any other time of the day, but at least once the sun starts going down in the sky you don't feel quite so much like an egg frying on a pan anymore. I stuck my arm out the window of Daddy's pickup and felt the wind play over it, still thick with humidity even when we were going nearly fifty miles an hour, trying to pretend like it was Thanksgiving time and I was sitting outside in the crisp chill of fall.

We'd been waiting four days for the tractor belt to come into Anton's store—four days when Daddy couldn't use the tractor at all. Finally, on Thursday evening, Anton had called Daddy and told him the belt had come in.

"I gotta drive over and pay for it after dinner," Daddy had said, "and hopefully I can get it in before dark tonight." He'd scratched the back of his neck and frowned a little. "Hope I can remember how to put it in."

"Ask Anton for a refresher," Mama said, wiping spaghetti sauce off Mylie's forehead.

"Yeah. I'll have to." Before Grandpa Kelly's stroke, he'd always been the one to do most of the repairs.

"Can I come with you, Daddy?" I asked.

Daddy shrugged and looked at Mama. "Long as that's okay with you, Suzie."

"Sure," said Mama. She didn't even have to nag at me to load up the dinner dishes, like normal; all week long, I'd been doing my chores and plenty of hers, too, giving her as much rest as I possibly could.

I just hoped it would be enough. I still couldn't think about Miss Tabitha and her magic honey without curling my hands into fists, so angry and sad I could scream. Surely if she'd *wanted* to help bad enough, she could've. Hadn't that Quigley honey been responsible for miracles in Maryville longer than I'd been alive?

I ducked into my bedroom and found the little blue book of poems by Emily Dickinson sitting on my dresser. I hadn't touched it since Saturday morning—every time

I saw it there in my room, it was like I could hear Mylie's screaming in my ears, see the blood where Mama had chewed her lip to the quick listening but not helping. I couldn't stop thinking about it, how I could've done more, could've been there when Mama and Mylie needed me.

It wasn't the book's fault, everything that had happened . . . but maybe it was mine. If I'd been faster with those eggs, if I'd been doing what I was supposed to and not sneaking in time to read poems I didn't even understand, maybe I'd have been fast enough to help get to Mylie before it got so bad.

Maybe I'd even have been able to talk Mama back into her right self, help her see how wrong her thinking had gone.

I took one last long look at Miss Emily's book and then slid it into my purse, zipping it up so I wouldn't be tempted to take it out again.

That purse was sitting on my lap now, bouncing a little when Daddy bumped the truck over a pothole. The weight of it felt secret and sad, like the time I walked into Arden's house and Miss Amanda was sitting in the living room crying, crying over the little black ultrasound picture of a baby that was never born. I'd snuck past her and gone right out the back door to find Arden, and never told either of them what I'd heard or seen. I wasn't sure why feeling the book resting on my knees gave me that same mix of shame and hot, teary prickles at the back of my throat, but it did.

The little box library was sitting out in front of the gas station just like the day Thomas put it there. I wanted to go over to it, run my fingers over all those spines again and see if any of the titles had changed, but I didn't trust myself to be able to put Emily Dickinson back in there without taking something else out. Tonight wasn't about getting a new book to read; tonight was about clearing up space in my head so that I could help Mama the way she needed me to, without being distracted by books or playing or anything else.

If I was going to fix Mama, it was going to take everything I had.

I followed Daddy over to the door of the Duck-Thru Food Store, but the light inside was turned off, and when Daddy pulled on the handle, it was locked. Daddy peered inside for a minute before noticing a little sign taped to the front of the door: *Please Come Around Back to the House*. Without a word, Daddy set off around the corner of the convenience store and down the driveway of Mr. Anton's small brick house.

Next to the house, wrapped in a small wooden fence

to keep the deer away (*Not that it helps that much*, Mr. Anton had told me once in a rueful voice), there was a little kitchen garden where collard greens grew high and tomato vines burst with bright red fruit. Old-timey wildflowers grew all around the path up to the doorway—blue bachelor's buttons and red poppies and pink and white daisy-looking cosmos.

Daddy only knocked once or twice before the door opened, Mr. Anton standing so tall I thought he might hit his head on the door frame.

"Miles! Come on in. Let me get my shoes back on and I'll go get your belt from the store." Mr. Anton's entryway was deliciously cool and dim, and the smell of fresh-cooked cornbread came from the kitchen. "Hey there, Della. How are you doing?"

"Just fine," I said, even though that was probably seven-eighths a lie.

"And how about Suzanne, Miles? She still feeling under the weather?"

"She's fine," said Daddy, sounding as casual as could be.

"Glad to hear it."

"You might have to refresh my memory on how to install the belt, Anton. I confess I've never done it by myself."

"Sure," said Mr. Anton, following Daddy. I didn't move.

"Excuse me," I said, blushing when both Daddy and Mr. Anton turned to look at me. "Um, is Miss Lorena here? I need to give her something." I hadn't told Daddy about the book sitting heavy in my purse. I didn't want him telling me to keep it.

"Yep," said Mr. Anton. "She's right through the hall and in the kitchen. Thomas is around here somewhere, too. Mind if I take your daddy over to the shop and get him rung up while you talk to her?"

"No, sir."

Miss Lorena was at the kitchen table, humming to the music, a bunch of papers and a thick book spread out in front of her. She looked up and saw me, that sunshine smile reaching all the way up to her eyes.

"Why, Miss Della Kelly," she said, putting down her pen and patting the chair beside her. "You come sit down here by me. Thomas tells me every day what good folks your family are. Y'all might make a farmer of him yet."

I sat on the edge of the chair, feeling the cool wood against the backs of my thighs, and slid the book of poems across the table toward Miss Lorena.

"You done with it?" She reached out for it. I shook my head and her hand paused, fingers spread out in the air above it. "Why you giving it back to me then, honey? It's yours as long as you'd like to keep it. It's one of my very favorites."

"Oh," I said, startled into being distracted. "Don't you want it back, then? Haven't you missed it?"

Miss Lorena chuckled. "Not a bit. I got another copy twice this big."

I snuck a look down at the little blue book. Miss Lorena's hand had drifted down and was sitting on it, her brown fingers soft and strong, but she hadn't pulled the book closer to her. It still sat there on the table between us, whispering promises.

"Besides," Miss Lorena went on, "I've got to spend all my reading time right now on classwork." She lifted her hand off Emily Dickinson and thumped the textbook on the table in front of her. "I'm sorry to say that when you are a grown-up and in college, there is no such thing as a summer vacation."

I stared at the textbook, its pages glossy and reflective in the evening sunlight falling from the kitchen windows. "You're in college, ma'am?" I'd never known anybody as old as Miss Lorena to be in college, or any kind of school, before; she had to be at least as old as my parents, maybe even older. Plenty of people in Maryville never even went to college.

"Yes I am. I chose not to finish up when I was young as most, and I've got to do my catching up now." She sighed, looking suddenly like a veil of sadness had drifted down over her, dimming the sunshine of her smile. "Back when I married Thomas's daddy, I was young and *so* in love. All I wanted to do was to spend my days taking care of that man. He had a laugh that could fill the whole world up and make everyone around him laugh, too. Thomas takes after him that way."

"What happened to him?" I asked, my voice hardly more than a peep.

"He died last year, honey. Cancer. His own daddy died of it, long ago, too. That's why me and Thomas moved down here—we needed a change, and Anton needed company, kicking around by his lonesome in this house."

"And so now you're finishing college."

Miss Lorena nodded. "I sure am. I'd like to be a teacher. An English teacher in a high school. Besides, all these classes keep my brain from getting lazy and forgetful in my old age."

I itched to ask her how old she really was, but swallowed the question back. Once, when I was pretty little, somebody's aunt was visiting Maryville and I was so fascinated by the contrast between her wrinkled skin and her movie-star yellow hair that I'd asked in the middle of the prayer at church if she was an old lady or a young one. Mama's eyes had popped open big as dinner plates, and she'd spent the whole ride back from church lecturing me on how you never, *ever* ask a woman her age.

Instead, I reached my own hand out to push *POEMS* closer to Miss Lorena.

"I need to give these back to you for a while," I said, sitting up so straight that my spine ran all the way up the side of the chair's back. "I'm not gonna be able to read them right now. But—"

I stopped, chewing on my lip.

"Yes?" Miss Lorena prompted.

"But I might like to borrow it again later," I said, voice mousy and small.

Miss Lorena looked at me for a long, long minute, her amber eyes turning golden in the window light. "You sure, honey?"

"Yes, ma'am," I said, trying not to look away.

"All right then," said Miss Lorena, slowly reaching for the little blue book and drawing it into her lap. Her thumb ran up and down the spine, tracing the black lettering without her seeming aware that she was doing it. "But I'm not gonna put it back in the box library. I'll tuck it away somewhere special, so that it's still there when you're ready for it, child."

"Thank you, ma'am," I whispered, wishing I was brave enough to say more than just that.

I'd stood up to go and find my daddy when Thomas came thumping down the stairs and into the kitchen, reaching his hands up to grab a glass from one of the cupboards.

"How's your studying going?" Miss Lorena asked, sliding her chair away from the table and standing up, too. She looked at me with a little bit of a laugh in her eyes. "We're a household of learning today, I guess. Here I am getting ready to write a paper while Thomas is studying to retake the SAT."

Her words were like warm honey, thick and sweet with love and pride.

"Hey there, Della," said Thomas, tap water frothing into his glass. When it was full, he drained the glass with a few big swallows and filled it right back up again. I watched, fascinated. How could one boy possibly drink that much water all at once, even if he was nearly as big as my daddy?

"I'm hoping to bring up my score so I can be eligible for more scholarships," Thomas said, setting the empty glass beside the sink and turning toward us. He wasn't anywhere near as tall as Mr. Anton, but he seemed to fill the kitchen anyway, all long arms and legs. Even just leaning against the counter, there was something about the way he stood that seemed different from most people—confident without being cocky or annoying, like he knew he didn't have a thing to prove to anyone but himself. The evening sunlight through the window over the kitchen sink highlighted his dark skin so it was almost golden.

"What he's not telling you is that he got a pretty near perfect score the first time," Miss Lorena said, smiling so much I swear she was brightening the kitchen all by herself. "But you've gotta be the best of the best to get scholarships to the places he wants to go. He isn't gonna let anything hold him back. My boy, the world will be hearing from him before long."

"Math is my cardinal weakness," Thomas said, shaking his head, but he was still smiling. "I'm trying to get my math scores up."

"Really?" The words pushed themselves out of my mouth without me trying. "Math is my best thing. I'd rather do worksheets all day than write a paper."

"Is that so?" Thomas asked, straightening up and reaching his hands behind his neck, stretching. "I guess I'll have to get you to tutor me sometime then."

I looked hard for a hint of a smile or a laugh, but Thomas seemed completely serious. Something warm and light spread all through me, till I thought I maybe could float up toward the ceiling like a birthday balloon, no string holding me down to the ground.

That floating feeling lasted all the way through the drive home and into the white door of the farmhouse, but then that balloon popped, and fast.

Mylie was screaming again when we came inside, yelling and crying just like she had Saturday when Mama had refused to get her up out of bed. She was standing in the kitchen, all naked except for her diaper, her orange hair matted to her head with sweat, and big fat tears were rolling down her cheeks and splashing onto her little white chest. In front of the refrigerator there was a brand-new bottle of ketchup, all squoze out and smeared across the fridge door, the cabinets, Mylie's hands.

Mama was on her knees on the linoleum floor, her yellow hair pulled up into a ponytail on top of her head that flew in every direction as she attacked the fronts of the cabinets with a wet sponge. The whole kitchen smelled of tomatoes and of bleach; it burned in my throat and made my eyes water.

"Suzanne!" said Daddy, his mouth moving like he didn't know anything else to say. In the light from the ceiling fan above our heads, his brown eyes looked big and black, and just as lost and afraid as I was feeling.

I didn't know if I'd ever be able to help Mama rest

enough to keep the schizophrenia from creeping back into her this time.

I was starting to think we were long, long past the time when it already had.

CHAPTER THIRTEEN

Before Grandpa Case died when I was eight, my mama was well enough to stay out of the hospital, but not always well enough to do much else. Sometimes she'd go all day long, sunup to sundown, without getting out of bed. Other times, she'd go for one or two or even three days in a row without ever sleeping more than a few hours at a time. Sometimes she heard voices talking to her that weren't really there—voices of people we knew or voices of people who only existed in her own head.

But mostly she did all right up until her daddy died.

Afterward, once she'd gotten home from that month in the mental hospital in Alberta, she went years without a single day where she heard things that weren't there or forgot how regular mamas were supposed to act. She was so healthy for so long I sometimes forgot that she'd ever been different from Arden's mama, forgot that she'd ever lived in a hospital where they locked the doors and only let Daddy visit once a day from three to five.

But then she had Mylie. And then this summer had come along, and the drought, and the watermelon seeds . . . and now, looking at Mama sitting there scrubbing at the cabinets with hands already turning red from the bleach, I didn't think that all the patience in the world would be enough to put things back to normal. This was so, so much worse than it ever had been before Grandpa Case died.

"Suzanne!" Daddy said again, the word cracking across the kitchen like a backfiring engine and making me jump, but Mama paid him no mind. She was in her own little world, a world of germs and voices nobody but her could hear. The rest of us might as well not have existed.

His jaw tight and hard, Daddy moved forward and picked Mylie up off the ground and washed the ketchup off her in the sink.

"Stop that," he said when he'd finished, catching Mama's hands and pulling her to her feet before prying the sponge away and tossing it into the sink. "You stop that right now, Suzanne. Listen to me. You hear me? You have got to pull yourself together!" He was holding Mama's hands—both of them together in one of his bigger ones—holding her so tight his knuckles were turning white. "Pay attention to your daughter, Suzanne! How long has Mylie been screaming? She needs you!"

Even with her hands caught inside his, Mama didn't look at Daddy. Her eyes were on the cabinet, like she could see those invisible germs dancing down them, undoing all her work.

"I gotta clean up, Miles," she whispered, her eyes roving up and down the cabinet in front of her, following the invisible line of the ketchup she'd already cleaned off, following the dancing germs only she could see. "I gotta clean up so the girls don't get sick. I gotta keep them safe, keep them from getting hurt."

Daddy let go of Mama all at once, so fast Mama rocked back on her heels. "The only thing hurting the girls is *you*," he said, and I wanted the heat to melt me right down into the floor, to fade out of existence and not have to feel the razor edge of Daddy's voice anymore. In my whole life, I'd never seen him like this.

Mama started crying, silent tears that rolled down her cheeks like raindrops. "I gotta do it, Miles. My daddy told me to."

Daddy spun around. "I can't take this anymore." His

face was red, and I couldn't tell if it was from the heat or the anger. "I gotta go fix that tractor belt before it gets dark. Della, take your sister."

He pushed Mylie into my arms—she was heavy and so hot she might have had a fever. Her thumb was in her mouth now, the sobs quieting down but the tears still pooling in her eyes and sliding down her baby skin.

The screen door slammed shut as Daddy stomped out, and a minute later I heard the door of the pickup truck slam, too, as he got out the part he'd bought from Mr. Anton earlier that evening.

How could Daddy just go out like that, leave me here with Mylie and Mama, not even staying around to make sure we'd all be okay?

Mama sank down to the floor, still crying, like Daddy had been the only thing holding her up at all.

I smooshed my lips together and took a deep breath in through my nose. My eyes were prickling and I wanted to cry, but Mylie and Mama were already doing enough of that for all three of us. Somebody had to stay in control, and for once it sure wasn't gonna be Daddy. I scooted Mylie over to my hip and stepped over to Mama, taking the spray bottle from the floor beside her and talking to her in a quiet, gentle voice, just like I'd used a few days ago to calm Mylie down.

"It's all right, it's all right," I said over and over again, but Mama didn't act like she'd heard me at all. She just kept on crying, not making any noise, her eyes puffing up and turning as red as her hands. I clumsily unscrewed the spray bottle and dumped everything inside it down the sink, my own eyes watering—it smelled like straight-up bleach, not thinned out with anything at all.

"You gotta wash your hands, Mama," I said, remembering what Mrs. Gregory had said last year in science lab about touching bleach, but Mama didn't answer. I reached into the sink and grabbed a washcloth off the faucet, running it under water till it was as cold as the sink could get it, and then crouched down and wiped Mama's hands off one at a time. It might not be enough to stop her hurting, but it was all I could do while still holding crying Mylie on my hip.

The heat of the kitchen pressed down hard on me, warming up that washcloth till holding it felt just like being wrapped up in the humid air. Mylie rubbed her face into my shoulder and whimpered, her arms holding tight onto my neck like she was afraid of what might happen if she let go.

"Stowy?" she whispered.

"Not now, Mylie." I wasn't sure I'd *ever* be ready to tell another Bee Story again. Instead I just held Mylie and looked out the window over the sink and wished, more than ever, that the sky would just open up and cry all the tears I couldn't.

That night I lay awake for hours, feeling the little trickles of air coming down from the ceiling fan and the bigger one from the box fan sitting in the open window, my thoughts louder than the cicadas outside. I had failed. I hadn't been able to get Quigley honey for Mama, hadn't been able to make her rest enough to heal, hadn't been able to turn any of my grand plans into reality. I had failed to be what Mama needed me to be—what *everyone* needed me to be—and now Mama was getting worse, and fast.

My skin prickled, goose bumps breaking out all over my arms even in that stifling heat. The way Mama was tonight—the way she'd been Saturday—I hadn't seen her like that since right after Grandpa Case died, when she was slipping away into a world where Daddy and I couldn't follow, and I was finding out what it was like not to have a mama at all.

I thought about the Bee Lady Sunday in church, telling me I was the one who needed fixing, not my mama, and squeezed my teeth together hard. How could she think that? How could *anyone*, after they'd seen my mama?

How could she have not even been willing to *try*?

And how could Daddy be the same way? Why had he just left me alone with Mama and the bleach earlier? Daddy leaving like that almost hurt worse than Mama acting the way she had. Daddy didn't have schizophrenia hammering at the doors of his mind; he didn't have any explanation for that except plain old choice. The farm was important, I knew, especially without calm, orderly Grandpa Kelly to keep things going smoothly. I'd heard in the things he'd said to Mr. Ben, to Mama, how ashamed Daddy would be if he couldn't keep Kelly Family Farm alive through this drought.

But how could the farm be more important than me and Mylie? How could it be more important than Mama?

I wished Arden was there. I wanted it so badly my stomach ached with it. On nights like these, I *needed* my best friend, needed somebody who had seen me and my family in good and bad for as long as I'd been alive, somebody who could tell me that things would all work out the way they had in times past.

But even if she had been here, would I be brave enough to tell her what I'd seen tonight?

Across the bedroom, Mylie stirred in her crib, whimpering a little in her sleep. I rolled over on my side, looking at her outline in the darkness, one hand curled around the crib bars, her head squeezed all the way into the corner of the crib. Only a baby could be comfortable like *that*.

I had no idea how I was going to do it, but as I lay there watching Mylie sleeping, so young she'd never remember what Mama was *really* like if I didn't make things better right now, I knew I had to try again.

CHAPTER FOURTEEN

I woke up the next morning drenched all the way to my sheets, my pajamas sticky and soaked against my skin. Both fans had stopped and the air in the room was so heavy I could barely breathe it in. The clock by my bed had gone dark, no green numbers smiling out at me, and I wanted to die right then and there.

The electricity had gone out.

Usually the power only cut in the summertime when a hurricane blew through, which happened pretty often—but this year all the storms had fizzled before they got this far up the coast, and we hadn't seen a drop of rain for months.

I peeled myself out of bed, leaving a big damp spot

where I'd been lying, and padded as quietly as I could over to my closet. Mylie was still sleeping, every bit as soaked through as I was, her wispy hair as wet as if she'd just taken a bath. I eased the closet door open and found my lightest, skimpiest sundress, and changed into it. Mama didn't like when I wore it; she always said it made me look like I was trying to be five years older than I was, and that children should wear clothes for children, not for teenagers. I'd pointed out at least three times that I was only one year away from being a teenager, and I definitely wasn't a *child* anymore, but mostly I left the dress hung up so we didn't fight about it. Still, a day this hot called for drastic measures.

Even all that bare skin didn't do a thing to cool me down, and I felt sticky and nasty. I would have given just about anything to spend the whole day standing under a cold shower.

I scraped my sweaty hair into a ponytail and wondered if Mama would let me cut my hair pixie-style, like all those actresses. Anything else was too much, in this heat.

Mylie whimpered again, louder this time, and when I looked over at her, she was sitting up in her crib, blue eyes big and teary. "Dell," she sniffled. "Ouchie!"

"Shh, little monster, it's all right," I said, running over and pulling her out before she could really get going.

She was slick with sweat, her pajamas sticking to her skin like papier-mâché on a piñata. I pulled them off and tossed them into a pile with mine. I got her diaper changed but didn't put any clothes on—sometimes it paid to be a baby. I wished I could run around in nothing but my undies today, too.

Mama was in the kitchen, fanning herself with the newspaper, looking too hot and bothered even to do the crossword. She had that faraway look in her eyes, like she was somewhere that wasn't quite *here*. I swallowed hard, feeling the heat drinking away all my energy and all my big plans, leaving me little and alone.

"Morning, Mama," I said, but she only grunted in reply.

Usually I got the eggs first thing, but this morning I needed something cold and I needed it fast. I strapped Mylie into her high chair and went to the fridge, reaching for the plate piled high with watermelon slices, just letting the cold air of the refrigerator wash over me for a minute.

"Close that door, Della," Mama snapped, and I pulled the plate out real fast and obeyed. I wanted to hold on to that cold watermelon plate forever, letting the chill sink into my skin, traveling from my hands all the way to my heart.

"Why's the power out?" I asked Mama. I'd never wished more for those useless, noisy fans to be running. Or, better yet, a fixed-up AC, working like it was meant to.

"Don't know."

"You want some breakfast, Mama?" I reluctantly set the watermelon plate on the counter, already imagining how sweet and cool it would be, and pulled down a box of cereal from the top of the refrigerator. I'd meant to cook a real breakfast again this morning—I'd try not to burn the eggs this time, and maybe boil some grits along with them—but no power meant no electricity meant no stove.

"Mm-hmm," Mama mumbled, still fanning away. Her eyes were closed now, her lips moving just a little bit, like she was off talking to somebody I couldn't see. Her face was squeezing itself into wrong-looking, upset shapes again.

I concentrated on pouring cereal into bowls for Mylie and me, so I didn't have to keep looking at Mama. Milk, too, in mine, but not in Mylie's—she was too messy for milk, and she liked the dry stuff just fine anyway.

"Mama," I said after a minute, as I carried the bowls carefully to the table and then went back for the plate of watermelon, "I'm gonna help you extra today, okay?

I really want to. I know I've still got to do my regular chores, but I've been thinking that maybe I could take Mylie with me when I go to the stand with Arden later."

Mama opened her eyes, her eyebrows halfway up her forehead.

"Arden babysits out there lots," I said all in a rush, before Mama could object. "She watches Rena and Charlotte out there all the time. Once Miss Amanda even let us keep baby Rowan for a while. Between me and Arden, we could definitely keep Mylie out of trouble."

I tried to sound confident and sure, even though I was the furthest thing from it: I knew full well the reason Mama had never made me watch Mylie at the farm stand was because Mylie was as much trouble as all of Arden's siblings put together. She'd probably spend the whole time toppling over boxes and throwing things.

Mama opened her mouth, the *no* resting right there on the tip of her tongue.

"And after we're done out there," I said, pushing my words out faster than Mama could, "during Mylie's nap time I could clean up the house. I could scrub everything real good, just like you do. That way you could rest and wouldn't even have to worry about the germs being all over anymore."

"I don't need rest. Don't know where you got that idea in your head, Della."

I wanted to say *You're supposed to be taking care of me, not losing yourself more every single day.* I wanted to say *You're never going to get fixed if you don't let Daddy take you to the doctor.*

I wanted to say *I need you, Mama.*

But I didn't. I just stood there for a moment, the watermelon plate cool and slippery in my hands.

"I just want to let your brain have a chance to get better," I said finally, my voice small. "Like Dr. DuBose says. You need rest, so you can get better."

In her high chair, Mylie tipped over her cereal bowl and watched the Cheerios slide onto her tray in a rush, giggling.

"There isn't anything in the world the matter with my brain," Mama said, words snapping like fireworks.

"But—"

"You listen to me, Della Kelly. It isn't your job or your place to sass your parents like this. I appreciate you trying to help, but there isn't any need. Nothing's wrong with me, child."

I wanted so bad to believe her, wanted her words to clear out all the fear and worry I'd been carrying for almost two weeks now. But I just couldn't. Not after everything that had happened. Not after Mama thinking she was talking to her dead daddy. Not after her leaving Mylie to scream and poop in her crib.

I set the watermelon on the table and left my cereal to get soggy and wet in its milk, and went to the cabinet under the kitchen sink, where Mama held her cleaning supplies. There was a spray bottle there called *All-Purpose Cleaner* next to a pile of rags. I pulled the bottle and a rag out and sprayed the faucet and the sink and the counters around them down real good, then started wiping, so careful that not a speck of anything was left after my rag passed by.

"Della Kelly, you sit yourself in this chair and eat," said Mama. "You know I don't like you doing that. You're not careful enough. And I'm sick and tired of everybody thinking I don't even have control over my own brain. Fact is, I've been feeling better lately than I have since Mylie was born." Her words slithered into me, making that worry roar even louder, making me look extra hard into her blue eyes, like maybe they could tell me all the secrets she was holding inside herself.

Daddy came in the back door then, stomping dust off his feet and kicking his old leather boots off onto the rug. He looked hot and tired, sweat glistening in the little rivulets on his face that were like baby wrinkles.

"Morning, Della," he said, coming into the kitchen and washing his hands off on a washcloth, leaving a big streak of brown dirt across the sparkling sink I'd just cleaned. All our water came from a well, so no power meant no more water, either, once we'd used up what had already been pumped. Usually Mama filled up every pitcher in the house as soon as the power cut, so we could make the best use of all the water that was left over, but I didn't see any sitting out on the counter today.

Daddy grabbed himself a bowl and filled it with cereal. "Power back on?"

"Nope," I said, and Daddy sighed, looking down at his hands, which were just about as dusty as when he'd come in.

"I'll call in and see if they've figured out what's the matter." Daddy reached for his cell phone and dialed the power company while he poured milk into his bowl. "Sounds like a pole got hit. The recording's saying power ought to be back online by this afternoon." He sighed, wiping his forehead with his shoulder. "Hope it's sooner."

"Me too." I grabbed a slice of watermelon and handed a second to Mylie. Today even the feeling of the juice dribbling down onto my thumb felt good—a tiny spot of sweet cool, even if it only lasted a second or two. I said a quick prayer that God would turn back on our power and maybe fix our AC while he was at it, and then kept my eyes closed and bit into my watermelon, relishing the explosion of chill against my mouth, all those crisp little membranes dissolving as I chewed.

"Della Cordelia Kelly," said Mama, voice sharp as knives, and my eyes popped open. Watermelon juice dripped down my chin, cool and sticky. "You put that down right now."

Mama was standing up, her newspaper forgotten on the table, and she'd grabbed Mylie's watermelon away from her.

Mylie screamed, squeezing her eyes hard until a tear popped out. "Mine! Mine!" she shouted, reaching up and trying to grab the watermelon back from Mama, but Mama held it up out of her reach.

"Suzanne, what's the matter?" Daddy's hand had frozen halfway to the watermelon plate.

"I don't want the girls eating these," said Mama, and she sounded like her throat was full of tears. Mylie's screams ratcheted up a notch.

"Suzanne," said Daddy, in that way that meant he was forcing himself to be calm when all he really wanted to do was yell, "give Mylie back the watermelon, please?"

"I don't want them eating these," said Mama again,

waving Mylie's slice. "Those seeds will get into their tummies and make them sick."

Daddy breathed in and out, hard, through his nose.

"That's ridiculous," he said, and I could tell he was about to lose it big-time. "There's hardly even any black seeds in that slice. Swallowing one or two won't hurt her."

I thought about bringing up the time Grandpa Case had told me that if I ate a watermelon seed a plant would sprout in my stomach and grow out my ears, but now didn't seem the time.

"Now," said Daddy, "give Mylie back her melon and let's sit down and finish breakfast. Have you taken your pill yet this morning?"

Mama shook her head, and Daddy took a tablet from her pill bottle and handed it to her. Mama sank back down into her chair, reaching for her glass of water and taking a big long drink, brushing something invisible off her shorts as she did so.

"Wait a minute," said Daddy. "What did you just do?" Mama didn't answer. "Suzanne, *what did you just do with that pill*?" Daddy's voice was going up and up, like a firework right before the blast.

Mama just sat there in her chair, staring at the newspaper in front of her, not saying a single word.

Daddy's whole body was quivering, and I swore I could feel the heat coming off him in waves, pulsing through the kitchen and sizzling everything it touched.

"Did you swallow that pill just now?" he asked. Even Mylie was silent, staring at Daddy with big scared eyes. I probably was, too. "Suzanne, *answer me!*"

Mama shook her head, a tight little movement that made her hair bounce. Daddy walked over to her, every step wound up like a clock, like it was taking everything he had to walk and not explode in a shower of sparks. When he got to Mama, he lifted up both her hands from her lap. The pocket of her shorts was smeared with white, where she'd rubbed her hand against it.

Ignoring Mama's attempt to bat him away, he stuck his fingers into her pocket.

A minute later, they came back out, holding that little white pill.

The kitchen was silent, quieter than it had ever been in my whole memory, not even the whir of the ceiling fan or the hum of the refrigerator to break it up. Even Mylie, frozen in her high chair, didn't make a peep.

From the Hawthorne farm, a rooster crowed.

Daddy let go of Mama's hands. They dropped, limp and lifeless, into her lap.

"I don't need those pills anymore, Miles," Mama

whispered, so quiet I could hardly hear it. "I don't need them. They make me feel funny. They make me fat and foggy. I'm better without them. I haven't been this clear-headed since Mylie was born."

Daddy's mouth worked up and down.

"Can't you see?" Mama asked, not whispering anymore. Her regular voice in that dead-silent kitchen sounded loud as a bullhorn. "Haven't you noticed? I'm myself again. I can see things, understand things, hear things I couldn't before."

Hear things like your dead daddy. See things like armies of germs crawling all over everything. Like evil watermelon seeds.

"All I've seen is you getting sicker and sicker," said Daddy, finally, the words tearing out of him. "All I've seen is you ignoring your kids and worrying all of us half to death. And now I'm seeing that you *did this yourself*? How long you been skipping your pills, Suzanne?"

Daddy was close to yelling now, and Mylie was crying again, big scared sniffles that sent snot rolling down her face. I hunched down in my chair, wishing I was anywhere else in the world.

"I don't know," said Mama. "Few weeks. Maybe a month or two. I knew you wouldn't understand."

Daddy reached for the pill bottle and shook another

pill out, holding it out to Mama. "Well, you start taking them again right now. You know what Dr. DuBose said! You know what a difference this medication has made for you, Suzie!"

He was begging now, the pill white and shiny on his hand, but Mama didn't move.

"I feel better without it," said Mama again, her chin set tight, her mouth a thin line. "I don't need it, Miles. There isn't anything wrong with me! Those pills *make* me sick."

"Are you even hearing yourself right now? You haven't been this sick in *years*!" Daddy was really yelling now, every word he said landing on my skin like acid, making my hands shake until my spoon was clattering against my bowl *ting-ting-ting*. I dropped it, but Mama and Daddy were too busy fighting to look at me.

"Damn it, Suzanne, this is *not* an okay time for you to lose it!" said Daddy, and my head shot up to look at him, my eyes big as melons. I'd heard Daddy swear a few times on the farm, when the bugs got into his squash or the tractor broke down, but I'd *never* heard him swear at Mama. Mama looked shocked, too, her mouth hanging open in a little round O.

Mylie's crying was starting to get louder, sniffling turning into little sobs, but I couldn't make myself move to stand up and get her from her high chair.

"Della, take Mylie outside," said Daddy without looking at me. "Go ahead and get started picking for the stand today."

My legs felt like noodles as I stood. Mylie stopped crying as soon as I'd gotten her up, and she buried her face into my neck, leaving a trail of snot across my skin. I didn't bother to find her shoes, just slipped on my flip-flops and opened the back door. As it swung shut, I could hear Daddy's voice rising again.

"I just can't take this stress on top of already worrying that I'm going to lose my daddy's farm," he said, and then the door slammed shut behind me.

I could hear Daddy's yelling in my ears all the way to the garden.

CHAPTER FIFTEEN

Mama and Daddy didn't say a single word to each other all through the rest of that day. They walked around and past each other, their silences bubbling up into thick walls that kept them separate even when they were in the same room, never meeting each other's eyes or softening the hard lines that were their mouths into something like a smile.

Daddy had disappeared onto the farm not long after breakfast, the tractor sending up clouds of dust behind him. By the time Mylie and I got back in from picking in the garden after breakfast, something that took me three or four times as long without Daddy's help and with Mylie's interference, Mama had gone into her room and shut the door halfway. When I peeked through the crack, I saw her in there, lying on the bed, holding a book but not turning any pages, like she'd given up on being a mother or a wife or anything else at all.

The power was back on, though, making the ceiling fan above Mama's bed lift her hair up in little wisps. At least that was something.

I got Mylie dressed and kept her with me all day, thinking dully that at least I'd gotten my way and Mama was resting. Not that it would do anyone much good if she kept throwing those pills away every morning, slipping them into her pocket like they weren't the biggest blessing that had ever come into any of our lives.

We were kept busy at the farm stand that morning, a steady stream of tourists and locals coming by. Between that and trying to keep Mylie out of the produce, Arden and I hardly had a moment to ourselves to really talk, which was a good thing. I didn't know how I could explain to her about Mama's pills—but I didn't know how *not* to.

We were halfway through our shift when the Bradleys' blue car pulled off to the side of the road and Miss Lorena and Thomas got out. Miss Lorena waved as they walked over to us.

"I've got to tell you, Della, that your daddy sent

Thomas home last week with some Kelly farm butter beans, and they were the *best* I've ever eaten." She closed her eyes and smiled, like she was remembering the taste. "I decided this morning that it was high time Thomas and I came by to see what other offerings y'all have got."

I grabbed the back of Mylie's shirt before she could tear out into the road. "All this stuff's from our farm or the Hawthornes'. That side over there's certified organic, too. Actually, all of it's pretty much organic right now, 'cause Daddy's been changing things over on our farm this year, but only the Hawthornes have got that thing from the government."

"Mmm," said Miss Lorena, running her copper-colored hands over a row of watermelons. There weren't as many as we normally had this time of year, with Daddy's melons fighting the anthracnose so that we barely had enough to eat ourselves and only the Haw-thornes' melons ready to sell, but the ones we did have were shining and green and sweet as ever. "It even looks beautiful. They don't have this kind of deliciousness in the middle of the city, let me tell you! Thomas, want to carry one of these to the car for me? How do I pick out the nicest one, Della?"

"Best way is to lift a couple of them and see which one feels heaviest. That means it's got the most juice. You can thunk them, too, but that's harder if you haven't got practice listening to them."

Thomas picked up three different watermelons in a row, looking so nervous I wanted to laugh, but he finally settled on one and carried it back to his mama's car.

"There is absolutely nothing better than cold watermelon on a hot summer's day. Watermelon is my very favorite fruit, I think." Miss Lorena gave a little half-sad sort of laugh. "When I was pregnant with Thomas—back when dinosaurs roamed, of course—it was in midsummer, and all I ever wanted to eat was watermelon. I was so hot and queasy all the time, it was the only thing that ever sounded good. Mr. Bradley used to joke that he wasn't sure if I was getting round because of a baby, or because of a baby watermelon."

"He sounds nice," I said. "And funny."

"Oh, Della, he certainly was."

"Watermelon's my favorite, too," I said, even though all my good watermelon memories seemed to be shot through right now with the bitter taste of Mama's watermelon-seed obsession. "They're like the taste of summer."

"The taste of summer, indeed. And you said you weren't good with words!" Miss Lorena cocked her head to one side. "I think you might have a poet's heart, Miss Della Kelly."

Mylie toddled over to the watermelons, wrapping her arms around the closest one and going red in the face with the effort of trying to lift it off its table. "Yum, yum!" she crowed. I jumped up.

"Put that back, baby, before you smash it to pieces!" I sank back into my camp chair and tried to hold her between my legs, but she squirmed and wriggled until she managed to break free.

"Seems like you got your hands full," said Miss Lorena as Mylie shot across the canopy and filched a green bean from its basket.

"Tell me about it," I said, but I let Mylie keep the green bean. She liked to chew on them and then spit the chewed-up mess all over the ground, but even that was better than her dumping out the basket or pushing her fingers into the peaches or any of the million other things I'd had to stop her doing so far this morning.

"Hey, Mylie baby," said Arden in a singsong voice, "Come play a game with me?" She held out her hands to Mylie.

"Little stinker," I said as Mylie shot past me and into Arden's arms. Just about everyone alive loved Arden, Mylie included.

As if they had appeared in response to my thoughts, five ladybugs flitted down from the canopy overhead and landed—one on each of Arden's hands where they wrapped around Mylie, three on the arm of my camp chair. Arden looked up at me and smiled, a secret smile that made me smile back.

Lucky ladybugs. For the first time since that morning, life didn't feel like it was pressing so hard against my forehead that it was giving me a headache.

Miss Lorena set a row of paper bags on the card table next to the till. "All right, ladies. I've got some butter beans, some green beans, a couple of bell peppers, and some blueberries." She looked at Arden and me in mock seriousness. "I confess I was tempted by the zucchini, too, but Anton's garden seems to be nothing *but* squash right now."

"Him and everyone else in town," said Arden. "Tourists are the only ones who ever stop for the zucchini. Trust me. People around here always say if you aren't careful you'll find zucchini stuffed into your mailbox, gardeners are so desperate to get rid of it."

"How much do I owe, with all these things and the watermelon?"

I closed my eyes, running through the numbers, then gave her the total.

"I'm thoroughly impressed," Miss Lorena said as she handed me her credit card and I swiped it through the card reader on Mr. Ben's cell phone. "I can't do mental math to save my life. Thomas doesn't fall far from the tree in that regard."

"It's the truth," said Thomas as he scooped up his mama's bags. "You started doing quadratic equations yet, Della? Every time I get to that part in SAT prep, it gives me a headache, I swear."

I nodded. "I'm in the advanced math class, so we started algebra last year."

"I'd be jealous if advanced math didn't sound like the worst thing I'd ever heard of." But I could tell from the way Thomas was holding his mouth extra-serious that he was laughing on the inside. "See you soon, Della."

I ducked my chin down so he couldn't see me smiling.

CHAPTER SIXTEEN

I was exhausted by the time Mr. Ben came to spell us off at the stand a little while before lunch, his white skin streaked with sweat and dirt. Keeping Mylie safe *and* out of trouble underneath that ten-foot-by-ten-foot canopy was a full-time job.

"Let's go to the playhouse," I said to Arden as I showed Mr. Ben the tally of our sales from that morning. I couldn't face Mama or Daddy yet.

I didn't want to see if Mama was still there, lying on her bed, pretending nothing was wrong.

"Sure." Arden took Mylie's other hand.

"Swing!" Mylie shouted, so we swung her up between us over and over again, until my arm felt like it was ready to fall off by the time we got to the playhouse. It was just the two of us and Mylie today, since Eli and Rena were playing inside the house—*they* had air-conditioning that actually worked—and Miss Amanda had taken the two littlest ones to the grocery store half an hour away.

I dropped Mylie's hand as soon as we got to the playhouse and flopped down on the ground, leaning up against one of the green plywood walls. "Ugh. I am *so* tired." Mylie danced off behind the playhouse, singing a baby-talk song to herself.

Arden sat down next to me, her shoulder rubbing up against mine. A pair of ladybugs buzzed through the air, red wings blurring in the sunshine.

"Me too," she said, stretching her legs out on the dusty dirt in front of us. "It's so *hot*. It makes everything feel twice as hard."

"Dell!" Mylie ran back to us, giggling, her hands stretched out. Green paint was smeared across them and dripping down her palms. She had green handprints on her dress, and her face, and her hair.

I shot up so fast I banged my elbow on the playhouse wall. "Mylie Alexandra Kelly!" I shouted, and Mylie took off running toward the bay, still laughing like a baby hyena. "Where did you even *find* that? You get back here!"

"No-no-no!" Mylie yelled, her fat little legs pumping. She was way faster than any sixteen-month-old baby ought to be. She ran right up to the edge of the water, keeping just an inch out of my reach the whole time, and then kept on toddling all the way until she ducked right under the surface.

"You little monster baby!" I hauled her out of the water by her arms. She was crying now, water streaming off her hair and her dress and making the green paint on her hands runny and wet. She wasn't coughing or choking, though, which I figured was a good sign.

Arden was cleaning up a puddle of paint from behind the playhouse when Mylie and I made it back there, Mylie already squirming in my arms and laughing again, like she'd forgotten all about being scared and sad.

"I don't even know how she got that paint bottle open," said Arden, taking the paint and stretching up on her tiptoes to set it on top of the playhouse roof this time, just in case. "I swear, Della, I'd rather have every one of my sisters *and* my brother all rolled up together than Mylie. Even Eli," she added. Eli was a pest and spent most of his time trying to spy on us and figure out all our secrets.

"Tell me about it," I said grumpily, putting Mylie in the playhouse and sitting in the doorway so that she couldn't get out. Mylie clapped her hands and then started rubbing them on the walls, leaving big smudgy streaks of green.

Arden sat back down next to me, giving me a sideways look. "What's up with your mama, Della?"

She'd asked me the same thing every day all week, and each time I'd changed the subject. I'd wanted so badly to be able to tell Arden that Mama was healed, fixed forever, that nobody had to worry anymore. Even though Arden had seen Mama at her worst, even though I'd told Arden myself that I thought Mama was getting bad again, there was something about speaking the truth aloud—like if I opened my mouth and said how things really were, I'd be giving up all hope of them getting better.

I think Arden guessed some of that, because every time I'd ignored her question, she'd let me do it. But there was something in her brown eyes now that reminded me of the way the O'Connells' milk cow looked when she didn't want to be milked, stubborn and prepared to stay that way as long as she needed to.

"Don't pretend you don't know what I'm talking about," Arden added, just like she knew what I was thinking.

"I think it's getting better," I said, but my voice

wouldn't come out quite right.

"Liar. I can see it all over your face. What's going on, Dell?"

I thought about Mama's pill, stark white on Daddy's hand that morning, but I couldn't bring myself to tell Arden about that. If I did, there'd be no going back at all, no chance I could convince Arden to keep on holding my secret.

"Okay," I whispered. "It's not getting better. But you still can't tell anyone, Arden! I still—she still might—"

I'd never seen Arden looking so upset. "Don't you see? You and your daddy have to wake up sometime and realize you can't do all this on your own! Look, I bet if we talked to my parents about it, they'd—"

"No!" My heart was beating so fast it felt like there wasn't enough oxygen in the world. I closed my eyes and thought of numbers. Counting by nines was always especially soothing, with all that symmetry. *Nine, eighteen, twenty-seven, thirty-six, forty-five.* "It isn't just Mama. It's Daddy, too. I've never seen him like this, not in my whole life. Like he's going to break down right in front of my eyes, the way his tractor did. It's scary, Arden. What if he decides he just can't take Mama anymore, and he just . . . leaves? What if you tell somebody, and they take Mama away, and Daddy decides he's done, too?"

Fifty-four. Sixty-three. Seventy-two.

"I don't think he would do that."

"Just promise. Promise me you won't tell anyone. Just give me a few more days."

Arden looked like she was one step away from being sick all over the ground in front of us, but finally she nodded. "Just for a few more days," she said. "But *only* a few more days."

That night as I was drifting off to sleep, I heard Mama and Daddy talking in the bedroom next to me. None of the words they were saying came through the wall clear enough to understand, but I could still hear the murmuring, the way their voices went up and down for questions or statements, the way Daddy's sounded more like a hum and Mama's more like a whisper.

They weren't yelling, this time. Just talking, sounding serious and loving just like they had a thousand other nights while I was falling asleep. I wondered if they were talking about what had happened at breakfast. Daddy didn't sound angry; I wondered if he was working on forgiving Mama for all those pills she'd been only pretending to take for who knows how long.

I sighed and rolled over. It felt like I had been split down the middle, like the yellow-and-blue sun Arden and I had drawn at the farm stand last week. One half of me was relieved that at least Mama and Daddy were talking, at least Daddy sounded calm. Maybe I'd been wrong about that secret fear I'd confessed to Arden this morning at the playhouse.

But the other half of me still simmered with anger, hot and thick as the drought that lay over us all.

I thought of the white powder smeared across Mama's pocket.

Daddy may have been working on forgiving Mama for all those pills she'd skipped, but I didn't know if I ever could.

And I wasn't sure I could forgive *him*, either, for forgiving her.

CHAPTER SEVENTEEN

The next morning I brought Mylie outside with us while Daddy and I were working in the garden. I was trying to pick blackberries—about as well as you can pick blackberries when Mylie is involved, sneaking green ones into your bucket and smooshing the ripe ones all over her hands and face—while Daddy did pest control, picking bugs off the potatoes and squash and spraying insecticidal soap on the aphids and spider mites. He muttered under his breath the whole time, all annoyed about a big nest of mites making a home in his herb garden, so that hardly any were getting big enough without ending up speckled with yellow spots.

"Ain't nobody wanna buy polka-dotted herbs for two

bucks a bunch," he said, cutting off a handful of yellowed mint sprigs and tossing them into a trash bag.

I didn't answer, just swatted Mylie's hands away from my bucket. She was trying to pilfer berries from my bucket to put into hers, and I didn't like having to pick twice as much for half as many.

I snuck a sideways glance at Daddy, where he was frowning over his row of basil plants, which were starting to sprout tall green flower stalks. Nobody had said a word that morning at breakfast about Mama being sick—but when Daddy had shaken one of Mama's pills out onto his hand and slid it across the table toward her, she'd pretended not to even notice, just chewed and swallowed her food like a machine, every bite the same size, never meeting my eyes or making a sound that didn't come from eating.

After breakfast she'd picked up her book and gone back into her bedroom and lain down on the bed, just like yesterday, the ceiling fan fluffing her hair like little wings around her head.

The air outside felt too thick and hot to breathe, though it didn't stop Mylie howling like a little baby wolf and stealing more blackberries out of my bucket. Her shirt was already covered in big, dark purple stains. Yesterday I'd snuck to the trash and tossed the dress she'd painted green. Mama and Daddy hadn't noticed, but I thought they might start suspecting something if Mylie's clothes kept disappearing at this rate.

Daddy rubbed at his forehead and stood up, stretching and yawning at the same time. He was at least ten years younger than Mr. Ben, but lately he looked nearly as old as Grandpa Kelly, his face sagging into exhaustion and his eyes painted with bruises underneath. I couldn't decide if I felt more sorry for Daddy or more angry with him. Shouldn't he have done more, held on to being mad a little longer, made Mama see sense and reach for that pill bottle again?

He looked over and caught me scowling, my hands resting on my blackberry bucket. A little smile slipped into his eyes, tugging up one side of his mouth just the tiniest bit, smoothing out all those lines and bruises.

"What's eating you, Della?" he asked, wiping sweat off his face. I was pretty sure that by the end of this heat wave all of Daddy's shirts would be just as ruined as Mylie's.

I looked away and picked a few more berries. The ripest ones came off their stems like a knife through butter, slick and easy. Mylie grabbed one beside me and popped it into her mouth, sucking all the juice out of it and then spitting the pulp onto my knee.

"Yuck," I said, rubbing the chewed-up berry off. It left a big purple track on my skin, slippery and wet. A bee buzzed past me, burying itself into a blackberry bush.

Daddy was still looking at me, his arms folded and his eyebrows pulled up into question marks.

I sighed, but I found my mouth opening anyway, the words wanting to be said, lining up like numbers in an equation. "You shoulda made Mama take that pill this morning." Those words hung there on the thick morning air, ballooning up between Daddy and me, so that neither of us even cared that Mylie had found a stick and started digging a hole in the dust between the blackberry bushes.

The smile slipped out of Daddy's eyes, and he rubbed at his forehead again. "I can't do that, sweetie," he said, and I knew he was doing his best to beam love over to me in little waves, but I wasn't ready to feel it.

"Why not?" I slapped away a skeeter trying to land on my face.

"Della, sweetheart, what else do you think I should have done—tied your mama down and forced the pill down her throat?"

I didn't answer.

"Honey, even if I could do that, I wouldn't," said Daddy, his spray bottle forgotten at his feet. "Your mama is a grown-up woman and she deserves our love and respect, even when she's sick. I've gotta let her have her agency, the chance to make her own choices—even if it's hard for me. Even if I don't like the choices she's making."

He looked down at his shoes, his eyes far away. "Even if it's making life harder for the rest of us."

All his words sounded squeezed and strained, like it was costing a lot for him to get them through his teeth, but I didn't care. It definitely wasn't hurting him enough, if he was still saying them. Otherwise, he'd find a way to *make* Mama change.

"Without those pills, Mama isn't anything. She isn't a mama. She isn't in her right mind at all. She's—" I stopped, took a deep breath. "She's crazy!"

"That's not fair, and it's not true or kind either," said Daddy sternly. "Pills or no pills, she's still your mama. She's still *herself*—it's just buried a little deeper. She's not crazy, honey, she's sick. You gotta understand, Della, as hard as it is for us, it's ten times harder for your mama. When she gets like this—it hurts her, honey, inside and out. More than it hurts either of us. She's struggling, and she needs our love."

He sighed, the reprimand going out of him, his shoulders and his face crumpling down till he looked like an old man again. "But I want you to know something. I told your mama this last night, too. I don't agree with the choices she's making right now, but the law says that if she's not willing to seek treatment, her doctors and I can't force her to get it unless she's threatening to hurt herself or somebody else. But if it comes to it, I'm ready to make other arrangements for you and your sister."

My breath came in short little jumps. What did Daddy mean, *other arrangements*? "You mean like—sending us away from home?"

Daddy's mouth tightened. "I hope not. But keeping you and your sister safe is my top priority, honey, and if it comes right on down to it, having you stay somewhere else for a little while might be the only option."

"But that won't make anything better!" I felt like my thoughts were spinning somewhere way above my body, hardly even noticing when Mylie squished a handful of ripe berries up against my cheek. "You can't do that, Daddy, you *can't*!"

Yesterday, I'd told Arden the thing that scared me most was the idea of Daddy walking out on us all—but now, squatting in the dirt with blackberry juice all over my hands and face, this new idea scared me even more.

"Della, hon, I don't know what's going to happen, but I do know that we're gonna get through it. And we'll still be a family, no matter what—even if your mama has to go back to the hospital, even if you and Mylie have to go stay with Grandma and Grandpa for a week or two. All right?"

I didn't answer.

"Della?" Daddy asked. I nodded, quick and sharp, my jaws glued shut.

With a giggle, Mylie scooped up two big handfuls of dusty dirt and dumped them, laughing, all over every single berry in my bucket.

Later, after we'd all liked to die of heat exhaustion working the farm stand, I put Mylie down in her crib for a nap. "Go to sleep," I ordered, handing her a big sippy filled with milk, but Mylie threw it to the floor outside the crib and started crying anyway. I minded Mylie plenty, but it was Mama who had the knack for getting her to take a nap.

"Go to sleep!" I said again, hoping that maybe Mama would hear Mylie and come take over. I picked the cup of milk up off the carpet and handed it back, but Mylie just threw it again, hitting me square in the forehead.

"Ouch!" I yelled, but that just made Mylie howl even louder.

"Dumb baby," I muttered, rubbing the place the cup

had hit. It was probably gonna bruise. I stalked off to the bedroom door and sat in the doorway for a few minutes, hoping maybe Mylie would calm down and decide to curl up and go to sleep.

She didn't. Instead, her screaming just got louder and louder until I felt like it was going to rupture my eardrums even with my hands over my ears, and I gave up and picked her back up out of the crib. When she finally fell asleep, curled up like one big wet hot patch on my lap, her shoulders were still shuddering.

I put Mylie in the crib a second time and wandered into the kitchen, filling myself a glass that was more ice than water. Mama's pill bottle sat there on the table, shining orange in the summer sunlight, glowing like it was trying to remind me just how badly my plan to fix my mama had failed. No matter what I said or did, she was just getting worse and worse, giving up and checking out and spiraling downhill so fast it made my breath catch.

At this rate, she'd be in the hospital by next week.

A memory swam into my mind—Miss Lorena sitting at her kitchen table Thursday evening, laughing and telling me that doing homework kept her brain from getting lazy and forgetful as she got older. My fingers tightened against the slick glass in my hand; I took another sip, feeling the cool water slip down my throat and settle into my belly. Outside the kitchen window I could see a plume of dust kicked up by Daddy's tractor as he drove through the peanut fields.

Maybe I'd been going about it all wrong. Maybe what Mama's brain needed wasn't rest—maybe it was the opposite. Maybe the only thing all my helping had done was keep Mama from needing to work her brain as much.

Maybe she was getting sicker so fast *because of me.*

I drank up the rest of the water as quick as I could, till my insides felt sloshy and full, and then set the glass in the sink and hurried back into my bedroom. My backpack was stuffed under my bed, where it had lain ever since I'd kicked it there after school let out in June. I pulled it out as quietly as I could and then turned it upside down over my bed: a math workbook, a spiral notebook that had bent in half and lost most of its pages, a bunch of gum wrappers, and a pencil case filled with colored pencils tumbled onto my sheet. In her crib across the room Mylie stirred and whimpered a little; I froze, but she stayed still after that.

I eased open the dresser drawer and pulled out a pair of shorts and two tank tops. If it was hot inside, it would be even worse out there—for a minute I hesitated, thinking about all that heat. But I couldn't stay here, following the breeze from the fans while Mama got worse and worse.

I had to do something, and this was the only thing I could think to do.

I rolled the clothes up and stuffed them into my backpack, then tossed the math book and a pencil after them. I wished I hadn't given the Emily Dickinson book back to Miss Lorena—I'd need something to think on besides Mama. I slung my backpack over my shoulder and opened the bedroom door, careful to go slow past its creaky spot.

The door to Mama's room was still half-open. I tiptoed past it, pausing only a second to peek inside and make sure she was in there, reading on her bed and ignoring the world, and then snuck a tube of sunscreen and a little bottle of bug spray out from under the bathroom sink. In the kitchen, three peanut butter sandwiches in little plastic bags went into the backpack, too, along with a plastic bottle filled with water from the tap.

I'd opened the fridge and reached my hand in to grab a Tupperware filled with juicy red watermelon bites, but at the last second I put it back down and took a couple of peaches and stubby little carrots, still all covered in dirt, instead. The sight of that watermelon just took me right back to yesterday morning. I didn't know if

I'd ever be able to eat watermelon again without seeing Mama's panicky face, hearing her nonsense talk about watermelon seeds, watching her slip that pill down into her pocket.

When I'd got my backpack all zipped up and over my shoulder I snuck back into my bedroom. I stood by Mylie's crib, watching her sleep, for a long minute. There were two fans in here, but even then she was so sweaty I could tell she was going to leave a big damp patch on the sheet. I wondered if Mama would even notice.

I reached my hand into the crib, resting my fingers just the tiniest bit against her back so I didn't wake her up. "Bye-bye, Mylie baby," I whispered, my words swept away by the breeze from the fans so even I could hardly hear them. "I know you aren't gonna understand why I have to leave. And I know it'll probably just make things harder right at first—but I've got to do something to help Mama get better, and I'm all out of other ideas. Maybe with me gone, she'll remember why she's got to be our mama."

Standing there, feeling Mylie's back rising and falling—gentle as butterfly wings—as she breathed, I felt a little drop of doubt creeping into me, making the backpack on my shoulders feel twice as heavy and the air coming through the bedroom window twice as hot.

Maybe this new idea wouldn't help Mama any more than the last one had. I thought of Mylie last Saturday morning, screaming and screaming in her crib, all alone and upset.

But the honest, deep-down part of me knew that even if running away didn't help Mama one bit, I couldn't bear to stick around and watch her keep on getting sicker.

"I'm sorry, Mylie baby," I whispered, kissing my fingertips and then pressing the kiss onto the top of Mylie's head. "I'll be back soon."

I went to the front door, just in case Daddy or Thomas were in sight of the backyard. The metal of the doorknob was cool under my fingers. I stood up as tall as I could, feeling that backpack pulling at my shoulders, and turned the knob.

The outside heat hit me like an oven, ten times worse than the hottest room in our house. The sun was bright today, shining down so hot and strong it felt like it was burning my skin already, everywhere it touched. Still, I took a deep breath and stepped out onto the porch, pulling the door shut behind me.

CHAPTER EIGHTEEN

I sat in the dirt in front of the playhouse, looking out at the deep blue water of the bay and wishing there was even enough of a breeze to ruffle my hair. I'd gone into the playhouse as soon as I'd gotten here, but the air was so hot and stuffy inside it that I dropped my backpack and came on back out, trying to find a place with enough shade that it didn't feel like the sun was cooking me alive.

It was funny: when Arden and I had started building the playhouse last summer, balancing plywood scraps together and hammering the nails so hard they went all bent and crooked, I'd been mad, because the only reason we'd decided to build ourselves a playhouse was to make up for the one we'd lost. Maryville was full of old falling-down buildings, along the highways and out in the back of everyone's fields, most of them left over from when North Carolina was tobacco farms far as the eye could see. They'd been drying sheds, made to hang all those bunches of tobacco leaves from the rafters till they dried out and turned into something you could smoke.

Our farm wasn't any different. Daddy said the Kellys stopped growing tobacco way longer back than even he could remember, but in the far corner of the peanut field there was one of those old barns, all gray from living who knows how long through the weather—and, as Mama said, always one good gust away from falling down. Daddy had been promising to go knock it down and take the wood to the dump since I was only a little older than Mylie, but it was one of those things he just kept not getting around to.

When Arden and I were ten, we snuck into the tobacco shed without any of our parents knowing and set ourselves up in there, bringing old broken-down folding chairs I grabbed from the trash can and a tablecloth Arden's mama had thrown out, and calling it our little house. The shed smelled like sweetness and dirt, all the beams stained with tobacco juice, and light and shadow draped over us from the holes in the walls and ceiling.

We played there for a whole year before anyone figured out where we were disappearing to.

When they did, though, there was a *reckoning*. My mama yelled and yelled, and my daddy went the kind of dead quiet that was almost worse than yelling, and Arden's parents sat her down in their living room and had a long conversation where they said lots of things like *we trust you very much, but* and *we know you're very responsible, but* and *dangerous* and *condemned* and *would be heartbroken if anything happened to either of you.*

My daddy swore he was going to tear that barn down for real this time, which he didn't, but Arden and I both got scared enough that we never went in even long enough to get our stuff out. Instead we built the playhouse, which creaked and groaned if the wind blew too hard and which our daddies were pretty sure wasn't much safer than the tobacco shed—but at least it was smaller, so maybe it wouldn't kill us quite so quick if it fell on us.

Now I was glad we'd gotten found out. This spot wasn't all that much farther from my house than our old tobacco shed, but it *felt* like it was, looking out over the still waters of the bay and hearing the loons that never seemed to make it over to our place. It felt like a different world than the one I'd left behind in my hot, hopeless house this afternoon, and right now, that was what I needed more than just about anything at all.

Arden came late in the afternoon, after I'd already been at the playhouse for a few hours—nearly dinnertime, by the grumbling in my stomach. I'd given in and opened up my bag of sandwiches and was finishing them off, warm peanut butter and sticky honey oozing down my thumbs.

"I've been looking for you *everywhere*, Della Kelly," said Arden, putting her hand on her hip and raising her eyebrows at me just the way she does when she's babysitting and Eli gives her sass. I felt my own eyebrows going down, down into deep frowns. Nobody who wasn't your mama or your own big sister was allowed to give you that kind of a look.

"Shoulda looked here first, then," I said, licking off the last of the honey-sweet peanut butter and tucking the empty Ziploc back into my backpack. I was feeling cranky, the heat so bad that my hair was nearly soaked with sweat, ponytail and all.

"*You* should have come to the house first to get me. Why didn't you?"

I hesitated, the words heavy on my tongue. I rooted around in my backpack and pulled out a bottle of water—warm now, of course—and took a drink so I didn't have to answer.

Arden waited, not saying a word, until I finally put the bottle back down. You couldn't play chicken with a girl who had four little siblings. She was still watching me with that expectant eyebrows-up, give-me-your-answer-young-lady sort of face; I wondered if her forehead was hurting yet.

"You said you'd been looking for me everywhere," I hedged. "You been over to my house?"

Arden nodded. "Your daddy was out in the fields and your mama didn't know where you'd got to."

"How were they? What were they doing?"

"Who, your parents?"

"Mama and Mylie."

Arden gave me a funny look. "Um . . . your mom was at the kitchen table, and Mylie was playing. Why? How long have you been out here?"

"A few hours, I guess." I bit my lip, looking down at the dirt underneath me. "I ran away."

"You *what*?" Arden scooted around so that her face was right next to mine and I couldn't help but look her in the eye. "Are you serious, Della Kelly? For one thing, that's a stupid idea. And for another, you don't think your parents will figure out you're here as soon as they realize you're not coming back? And what about your mama? She definitely hadn't realized it yet. She'd have been in full-on panic mode if she had. Doesn't that worry you even the tiniest bit?"

I chewed at the inside of my cheek, wishing I felt as confident as I had a few hours ago when I'd packed up my backpack and slipped out the front door of my house.

"I can't go back yet. A couple days ago I was over with my daddy at Mr. Anton's house, and Miss Lorena was there. She told me something about how exercising your brain is important when you get older—it stops you forgetting stuff." I looked past Arden, out the door of the playhouse and to the blue water of the sound, trying to ignore the doubtfulness on her face.

"I don't know, Della. I'm not sure that's true for your mom. Isn't schizophren—"

"It's true. It's got to be true. I've tried everything else, Arden," I said, watching a line of geese flying high up over the bay. *Everything.* Even the Bee Lady and her useless honey. "You gotta believe me about that."

"I just don't feel right keeping the secret for you. And how long are you planning to stay here, anyway?"

I hunched my shoulders up, half shrugging, half curling into myself to try to hold off those tears from coming. "Maybe a day or two. But see, it's already working! You said Mama was out of bed and watching Mylie. She hasn't done that for two days!"

Arden still looked worried, but at last she sighed and nodded. "I guess so," she said, picking at her nail polish the way she does when she gets upset. "Though I still don't really feel right about it."

"Thanks," I said, relief running its way through all my skin cells, right down to my fingertips. "I'll make it up to you, I promise. And it won't be too long. I hope."

CHAPTER NINETEEN

The sun didn't set for hours after Arden left, and even when it started to drop down, the humidity kept everything just as hot as ever. My tank top had been damp so long I almost didn't notice it now. The mosquito bites, popping out up and down my legs even after I'd sprayed enough bug spray on myself that I'd ended up choking on it, were harder to ignore.

It was so quiet out here, without Arden to talk to, without Mylie screaming or Mama yelling or the murmur of the TV in the background. The only sounds were the lap of the water up against the bank and the calling of birds—sharp cries from seagulls as they sailed way above the bay on bodies that looked too light to live, deep throaty cooing of the doves that roosted in the trees and flew down to hunt bugs from between the rows of corn and wheat. Every now and then rainless thunder grumbled, so far away I thought I might've imagined it.

After a while, I pulled out the math book and started working through some of the problems. It was a book full of timed quizzes that we'd used last year, in sixth grade, and even though I didn't have a watch or anything to time myself with, feeling the scratch of my pencil across the worksheet helped me to sink into the deep, calm place I went when I took a quiz in school. My breathing got slower, my shoulders relaxed, the hard, scary things about the world faded around me.

The lightning bugs started appearing just as the sun was going down, sending fingers of orange into the sky over the bay. First one firefly, then another, then a dozen all flitting through the air around me, blinking their yellow lights like stars caught a few feet above the ground. I pulled my knees up to my chest and wrapped my arms around them, watching the lightning bugs dance, and for the first time all week I felt like my heart was opening up just a little bit. All around me the sounds of cicadas and little tree frogs and crickets grew, their song louder as the sun got lower.

Later, after the sky had deepened into navy, I saw a bigger light bobbing up and down and up and down way across the field. It came closer and closer until I could see that it was Daddy with a flashlight—heading toward Arden's house.

It took ten minutes to walk from the bay to the Hawthornes' house, but I could still hear Daddy's knock on the door clearly through the night stillness. I couldn't move. The air was heavy on my skin, prickling the hairs up and down my arms the way it does before a lightning storm.

It seemed like a whole lifetime before I heard the Hawthornes' back door creak open and saw Daddy's flashlight bouncing toward me.

I scrambled into the playhouse as the sound of Daddy's footsteps got nearer, but it didn't take him two seconds to walk around to the doorway and shine his light right in. I blinked, my eyes dazzled by all that brightness.

"Della Cordelia Kelly," Daddy said, his voice rough as the playhouse plywood itself, "you come on out of there and get yourself home this minute."

My body twitched, like it was getting ready to mind him whether or not my own brain told it to, but I stayed put.

"You hear me, Della? This ain't a joke. Come on out of there now."

"No," I said, my fingers curled into fists.

Daddy dropped down into a crouch, and when he spoke again, I could hear just how hard he was trying to keep his temper. "Della. Come. On. Home. Now."

I thought about crying, half because I felt like tears and half because I thought it might make Daddy feel sorrier for me, but couldn't.

"I can't." I realized when the words were out of my mouth that it was the honest truth. Whatever the reason I was out here at all—to help Mama, or to help myself—the thought of going back was even worse than the thought of staying out here, with the heat and the skeeters and the unfamiliar sounds off the bay.

"Della, honey, please come on home with me. You can't sleep out here."

"I have before!" It was the truth—Arden and I had camped out here once, near scaring ourselves silly imagining what could be out there in the dark beyond the playhouse walls.

"That was different. It wasn't just you alone. And Ben and I were probably wrong to let y'all do it in the first place. But you gotta come with me now, baby. Your mama thinks you've been at Arden's this whole time— she'd be terrified if she knew the truth."

"Tell her I'm sleeping over." I bit my lip. "I can't come home, Daddy. I just can't. It's too—" I thought of Mama sticking that little pill in her pocket, thought about Daddy saying he'd send Mylie and me away if things got too bad. "I just can't."

Daddy sighed and raked his free hand through his hair. When he spoke again, his voice was quiet. "Things've been hard for you lately. The last two weeks, especially. Right?"

I nodded.

Daddy stood up and kicked at the wall of the playhouse. I jumped. But in the flashlight glow, I could see that his face didn't look mad, just thoughtful, like he was testing the playhouse out.

I waited.

Finally, Daddy crouched back down to my eye level. "I guess this old shack will be safe enough for one night."

Not one single hair on my whole body moved. I hardly even breathed.

"Tell you what, Della," Daddy said, and now all the anger was gone out of his voice and he just sounded so, so tired, like he'd been alive for a thousand years and never slept a wink. "I'll make you a deal. You can sleep in here tonight—if you're really *sure* it's what you want, honey, it's hot as Hades out here—and I'll tell Mama you're sleeping over at Arden's. I'll come collect you tomorrow morning before church."

"It's what I want," I said real fast, before I could lose my nerve.

Daddy stood. In the dark night, holding the flashlight, he looked like a shadow, hardly there at all. "Sleep well. I'll be back in the morning."

He turned and went back across the fields toward our house, the flashlight beam swallowed right up in that black velvet night.

I curled up in the hard-packed dirt with my backpack under my head, trying not to think about anything: not Daddy's exhaustion, or Mama, or Mylie sleeping all alone in our room for the first time ever. Not about the thunder that still growled way off almost out of earshot. Not about last week, when Arden and I had found a huge hairy wolf spider in a corner of the playhouse.

Arden's little sister Rena had nightmares, sometimes, the kind that would send her straight out of bed screaming her head off in the middle of the night. It got so bad a few years back that Miss Amanda started getting a special kind of honey from the Bee Lady, and as long as Rena had a little spoonful of it before bedtime every night, the only kind of dreams that came her way were the good ones.

I wished I had some of that sweet-dream honey right now.

I tossed and turned for a long time before I finally fell into a hot and restless sleep.

When I woke up the next morning I was stickier and dirtier than I could ever remember being. It was a little like waking up after camping, except that even the few times we'd gone camping together as a family I hadn't been sleeping right on a floor made out of dirt. My skin was tacky and gritty all over—when I blinked, even my eyelids felt dusty.

I groaned and sat up, not sure whether my arms and legs itched more because of the dirt or because of the puffy pink mosquito bites underneath it.

It was early. Out the playhouse door, I could see the sun still hanging low over the silver bay, barely beginning to push its light past the trees that lined the edges of the Hawthornes' farmland. Away off on the road I could hear the sound of a car passing by.

When would Daddy come for me? A little part of me whispered that I should just go, pick up my backpack and run back over the fields to home without waiting for him, but I couldn't make myself do it. The thought of maybe seeing Mama there, lying in bed, staring up at the ceiling fan like she could see God—or maybe her dead daddy—in its swirling, was still too much to take.

I pulled out the math workbook from my backpack and popped up the lead on my mechanical pencil, but even numbers couldn't keep my mind away from thinking today. The heat came on as the sun pulled farther away from the horizon, until I was sweating so bad that the skin around my eyes stung with salt, so I closed them.

Lying there in that playhouse with my eyes closed and the nearest sounds the loons loo-hoo-ing out on the water, I felt about as alone as I'd ever been in my entire life.

I was so hungry I was starting to feel dizzy with it when Arden appeared in the playhouse door, a bag with four blueberry muffins in her hand.

"It's about time," I said, sitting up quick and grabbing a muffin from her before she could even say hello.

"It's barely past eight," said Arden, dropping the bag in the dirt next to me and sitting down. "Good grief, it's hot. Doesn't it make you want to, you know, go home?"

I looked down at the dust on my flip-flops. "How'd my daddy know I was out here last night?"

"I didn't tell anyone, I promise! Your daddy came over to my place after it got dark last night. He said you hadn't come home at all that afternoon, and Mom said you hadn't been over to our place at all. Your daddy looked right at me and asked if I'd seen you. I said no, but he knew I was lying. He said he guessed you were off in that playhouse."

"He say anything to your parents about my mama?" Arden shook her head.

I sighed, wiggling my dusty toes. Arden and I had given each other pedicures two or three weeks ago, with lime-green polish and little white starfish stickers, but the stickers had peeled off days ago and the polish was chipping around the edges.

"I can't believe he let you stay out here all night," Arden said.

I shrugged. "He didn't want to."

"So—" Arden paused, chewing over what she was going to say next. "When are you going to go back home?"

I could feel what Mama called my "stubborn face" cementing itself into place: teeth together, jaw locked up tight.

"What's the point in staying out here any longer, if your parents know where you are anyway?" Arden pressed. "I mean, you've got to be tired, right? And hot." She pushed a lock of sweaty hair off her forehead.

"She's gotten worse so fast, and I tried everything I

could think of to fix her, but none of it worked," I said finally, my voice hardly making it past my throat and leaving my words mangled and soft. "Without me helping, maybe . . . maybe she'll run out of options."

Arden picked at her nail polish. "Don't you think you being gone might . . . make things worse? Doesn't your mama worry an awful lot about you when she's sick?"

"I can't go back," I whispered. "I can't. Not yet."

I wasn't ready to see Mama again. Not to see the mama I'd left, anyway, the one who just lay in bed like she didn't have a family. Right then, I ached so bad for the mama who sang songs and read books and used big words that the ache liked to swallow me whole.

Arden was quiet for a long time, her forehead creased up like a bedsheet after you'd slept in it.

Finally she stood up slowly, her ponytail only an inch or two below the rough plywood ceiling of the playhouse. "I've got to go back up to the house. Mom and Dad will be needing my help with the kids. You could come, too, you know."

For a moment, I thought about a kitchen that smelled of fresh blueberry muffins, about the way it sounded when Rena and Charlotte giggled, about *air-conditioning*. My toes scooted, just a little, like they were getting ready to stand up, too.

But then I imagined Miss Amanda opening up her arms for one of those big mother-hugs like I hadn't had since before the wrongness started taking up residence in my own mama's brain again—and my feet froze, rooted to the dirt of the playhouse floor.

Somehow, the idea of that hug almost hurt worse than being out here all alone.

"No," I said. "I'll stay here awhile longer. Till my daddy comes."

Arden sighed. "If you say so."

The wind picked up as she disappeared around the corner of the playhouse, howling all around me, a voice so sad it filled my throat up with tears.

CHAPTER TWENTY

That morning dragged on and on. By the time the sun was halfway up to the top of the sky, it was so hot I had to crawl out of the playhouse again and sit, miserable and stinking like sweat, in the shadow of the wall, eyeing the sparkle of Hummingbird Bay and wishing more than ever that I'd brought a swimsuit.

The sky above me was moody, with thick stacked-up gray clouds that blew across the sun like sailboats. The wind was whipping my hair around my face and the thunder that had been whispering when I went to sleep the night before was booming now, some of the claps so big I could feel them echo up through my skin—but there wasn't a single drop of rain. The playhouse quivered and quaked where I leaned against it, trembling in the wind like it was afraid of what the storm might bring.

All those storm clouds did was hold the heat in over me like a blanket on a hot summer night, till it was too hot to do anything but just lie there, staring out at the bay and wishing it was chilly midwinter and I was home, with Daddy beating me at checkers and Mama singing a song to Mylie. Daddy always says Mama's singing voice is so sweet it can call the birds down from the trees, and it's true—once, a long time ago, I came outside to where Mama and Daddy were fertilizing the corn and saw the fields all covered with birds who'd flown down to hear Mama singing as she worked.

That was the Mama I missed. The singing Mama, the Mama who'd read every single book of Harry Potter to me when I was ten and done all the voices, too, the Mama who told the lamest knock-knock jokes I'd ever heard and then laughed so hard afterward that she cried.

I kept glancing over to where my own house sat in the distance, wondering when Daddy would come marching over and tell me it was time to get on home. Was Mama better? The same?

I couldn't let myself wonder if she might be even worse.

I chewed on my lip, watching so hard my eyes started to water.

It was past time for church to have started, I was sure of it. Way past time for Daddy to have come. My whole body buzzed on high alert, my ears straining for any sound that might have been Daddy.

But the only sounds in all the world, it seemed, were the sounds of the bay and that rainless thunder, rumbling up all the way to my scalp.

When Daddy finally came, his outline smudged and blurring in the heat haze as he strode toward the playhouse, I nearly collapsed in relief. I stood up real fast and waved, a smile creeping up onto my face for the first time in days.

I could feel it deep in my bones, that relief, a quiet whisper that things were mending themselves back to just the way they ought to be.

That feeling lasted exactly as long as it took Daddy to get near enough for me to see his face. There was a story written there that I couldn't read—something a little sad and a little anxious that made my fingernails curl in so that they dug into my palms.

"Sweetie," he said when he got close enough I could hear him, but I couldn't say anything back. My tongue had forgotten how to work, right along with my heart and my breathing. Every part of me was still, still as the bay on a glassy-calm day, so motionless I might have shattered with a touch.

"Della," Daddy said with the kind of quiet grown-ups have when they're about to give you bad news, "I need to tell you something."

I would have swallowed, or chewed my lip, or pulled my gaze away from Daddy's, but not one cell anywhere on my body would listen to me when I told them to move.

"Your mama got pretty bad this morning. I had to call an ambulance, honey. They just left a few minutes ago, to take her up to the hospital in Alberta."

The world burned up around me. My head spun with the heat until all I could think was *rain, rain, rain*, over and over, my mind so crowded with wishing for rain that I couldn't spare a single thought for Mama. In the hospital. *The mental hospital.* In Alberta. Taken over by the schizophrenia until she wasn't anybody's mama anymore.

My eyes were so dry they felt like they'd got dust in them. Shouldn't I be crying? Shouldn't I be asking questions? Shouldn't I be standing up and running up the highway as far as my legs could take me, running after that ambulance that was already driving Mama away from us?

"I'm so sorry, Della baby. I know this is what you were afraid of. I wish I'd had any other choice. She wouldn't let Mylie eat, honey. She spent all morning keeping every bit of food or milk away, and I didn't know till I'd come in from my chores. She kept shouting that she didn't want anything to hurt Mylie, didn't want anything to make her sick. When I tried to give your sister some breakfast, Mama scratched and hit and even tried to bite me."

The hurting in Daddy's voice was the worst thing I'd ever heard, so sharp it cut into me the way a shovel slices through dirt.

"I tried, Della. I tried to help her, but I just couldn't."

"Why'd she do it?" I asked finally, my voice reed-thin and trembling. A hot gust of wind wrapped itself around me, pelting my legs and arms with little grains of sand and dust, a hundred little fires on my skin.

"She didn't mean to, honey, I promise. She just—" Daddy stopped, his face all crumpled into itself. "It's her sickness. It puts wrong beliefs into her head, ones she can't shake no matter how hard she tries. She believes that you and Mylie are in danger—from germs, from bad people, from just living life itself. She worried about you, being gone. Even when I told her you were at Arden's, she worried."

Daddy rubbed at his forehead. "I've got to head up

to Alberta as soon as I can so that I can talk to the doctors who are gonna be admitting her. I'm taking Mylie up, too, and we'll both stay at Grandma and Grandpa's house tonight. The doctors will be spending today getting Mama settled down and comfortable, but she might be ready for visitors tomorrow or the next day. If you want, you can come stay at Grandma's house, too, and go with me to visit Mama just as soon as we can."

You had to be twelve to get a visitor's pass to the unit they'd taken Mama to before, so in all those weeks when she'd been locked up in the hospital, I couldn't see her. Still, I remembered the visiting hours as well as if they'd been tattooed on the back of my hand: three to five p.m., the times Daddy had left me with his parents every afternoon to go hold Mama's hand and try to get her to remember who he was.

"Della?"

"No," I said, the word whispering out of me to hang in the hazy air in front of us.

Twelve years old or no, I couldn't do it.

Daddy nodded, like there was nothing wrong with me confessing I didn't want to see my own mama. "If you'd rather stay here, Miss Amanda told me they're happy to have you stay with them as long as you want."

"No," I said again.

"You gotta choose one, Della. You can't keep on staying down here in the playhouse all by yourself. I need to know somebody's looking out for you, even if you don't come up to Alberta with me today."

I thought of the noise and bustle at Arden's house— the little girls screaming and chasing each other, Eli and Arden fighting, the baby crying. Maybe Mr. Ben would pull out his ukulele and sing "Clementine" and "Down by the Bay" to keep the little ones entertained. The Hawthornes didn't have a TV, but it was always twice as loud and twice as fun there as at our house, even without one.

Being bored or lonely all by my own self seemed better than trying to hold myself together in all that happy at the Hawthornes' house.

"I just want to stay here," I said. "Or go home."

Daddy's jaw tightened up impatiently. "That's not even legal, honey. I can't leave you here for a whole day and a night and another day without an adult to look after you.

"Besides," he added as another gust of wind blew past us, rattling the plywood boards of the playhouse, "this shack is so unsafe Ben and I should never have let you girls build it. I can't believe I let you talk me into leaving you to spend a night here at all. Now it's time to buck up and come on over to Arden's, or with me up to Alberta."

"I don't want to," I said, not sure why the idea of being around people again made me want to cry more than knowing my own mama had just been picked up by an ambulance. Behind me, the playhouse creaked and swayed. "I just want to be by myself."

Heat lightning crackled against the horizon, and the wind blew even stronger, pushing against the playhouse till you could see it leaning hard sideways.

"What the—" Daddy started to say, his words snatched away by the gust, but he couldn't finish.

With one loud groan and a couple of *snap-snap-snap*s that made my ears ring, the playhouse collapsed.

I coughed, my mouth and lungs full of the dust it had kicked up as it hit the ground. The back of my right leg had a big old scrape from where the plywood roof had caught my skin as it went down; I could feel warm blood trickling down to my ankle.

"See?" Daddy said, his face as pale as the downy white heron that lurked in the shadow of a tree by the water's edge. He stepped forward in one big stride and wrapped me up in his arms. "You better thank the Lord you weren't in that thing just now, Della."

I wasn't sure who was shaking more, me or him.

"You sure you don't want to come with me?" he asked, and I could feel his breath on my wind-whipped hair.

Even now, not ever wanting Daddy's hug to end and with my heart still jumping from the shock of the playhouse falling over, I couldn't make my legs want to move. I shook my head.

"All right, then," he said, sounding like he wished he could change my mind. "I'll walk you on up to the Hawthornes' before Mylie and I take off. You'd better get that leg of yours cleaned up."

CHAPTER TWENTY-ONE

After I'd said good-bye to Daddy, Miss Amanda hugged me close to her, not seeming to notice or care that I was as stiff as the trunk of the apple tree outside their kitchen window. It was all I could do not to squirm away. I loved Miss Amanda so much she might as well have been my second mother, but right now, her hugging me felt exactly how I'd been afraid it would last night. All it did was hammer into me that it wasn't my own mama there with her arms around my shoulders.

"I'm so sorry, Della," Miss Amanda whispered. Over her head, I could see Daddy disappearing in the direction of my house.

Once, when I was seven or eight, I'd had the flu so

bad it felt like it would char me into a pile of ash. Mama had sat beside my bed all night long, switching out cool washcloths on my forehead and running her fingers through my hair, gentle as a whisper. Miss Amanda's words felt like those fingers—featherlight and so full of kindness and love it almost hurt.

"Would you like to talk about it?" Miss Amanda asked. Behind her glasses, the fair skin around her eyes was crinkled up in concern.

I shook my head. What was there to say?

She held me for a long moment, even though I hadn't reached my arms back around her. When she finally pulled away, her eyes were bright, like there might be the smallest sparkle of tears in them.

Arden hugged me, too, and I managed to hug her back, but not to get my tongue unstuck. All that long, hot day I stayed silent, listening to the thunder that rumbled along the edges of Maryville, watching as Mr. Ben drove his pickup through the field to load up the splintered plywood that had been the playhouse and take it to the dump. I stayed so small and quiet in Arden's big and noisy family that I went pale and light, like fog. I choked down lunch and dinner, and when the sunset had flamed red against the front windows of the house and Miss Amanda told me and Arden that it was time to get ready for bed, I didn't say a word.

There were already sheets on an extra mattress on the floor by Arden's bed for me to sleep on. The little girls had gone to bed hours before, their heads pressed together as they slept on the other side of the bedroom now—sleeping was the only time Rena and Charlotte could go two minutes without fighting.

"I'm glad you're here, Della," Arden whispered after we'd both climbed into bed.

"You're *glad* I'm here?" The first words I'd spoken all day long pulled out of me. Dry wind howled louder around Arden's house, like it was looking for a way inside.

"I don't mean it like that," Arden said quickly. "I'm not glad your mama had to go to the hospital. I'm not glad for any of that. I'm just—"

"I hate it here. I wish I was home." I curled my fingers around the edge of my sheet so hard I could feel the press of my nails through the fabric. "You don't get it, Arden. You don't get it at all. Your family is so *perfect*, and nothing bad ever happens to y'all."

It was mean, I knew it. Still, right there in that dark bedroom, I was so mad I could feel it dripping all down my skin like a red blush, hot and painful. Outside, thunder boomed.

"You think I don't know what it's like to have a family that sticks out in this town like a sore thumb?" Arden asked, forgetting to whisper for a moment. Charlotte stirred and whimpered on the bed on the other side of the room.

"It's not the same."

"But it's still hard!"

I was sure that any minute my skin would light on fire, burned up by the anger boiling my blood. My whisper voice was like a snake, sharp and hissing. "I can't believe you'd even say that. You couldn't possibly understand what my family is like, Arden Hawthorne."

"I'm *trying* to understand! But it's awfully hard to do that when you and your daddy are so darn proud you won't even tell anyone else in the world what's going on with your mama. Do you have any idea how hard it was for me to keep that secret for you? Do your grandma and grandpa Kelly even know?"

I didn't answer.

"Didn't think so," Arden said.

After a long, long minute where neither one of us said anything at all, she turned around and pulled the sheet up around her shoulders, even though it was hotter in there than the air-conditioning could possibly fix.

There was a Bee Story that Mama had told to me, and

that I'd told to Mylie, at least a dozen times. It was about two sisters who went everywhere together, as much a part of each other as the leaves were a part of the trees. Except one day they quarreled over something—and that argument got so big and so sharp that it took up more and more space between them, till they couldn't even go near each other anymore. They'd gone on like that for years, until one day somebody had given them a jar of Quigley honey, and the honey had filled them both up with so much sweet happiness that they couldn't even remember why they'd fought in the first place, and that big sharp thing between them poofed right out of existence.

I'd known Arden my whole entire life, and never once had any words come between us that felt as hard and hurtful as the few we'd just exchanged. Lying there on that mattress, I felt the fear of it creeping over me like the kudzu that twined over the trees beside the highway. If I didn't have Arden, I'd be like one hand without the other, broken off and incomplete, only half of myself.

I lay awake for a long time, listening to the wind and the thunder take turns trying to be the loudest, howling around the house without a single drop of rain.

I woke early the next morning, when the sky outside was still gray-purple. The wind had gone away during the night and left the air around Arden's house flat and lifeless, but the thunder was still out there, rumbling off at the corner of the world like a broken promise.

I slipped off my mattress and out of Arden's bedroom. I could hear Miss Amanda murmuring to baby Rowan in her own room, but all the lights were off and nobody else was about. It was strange, being here all by myself in the barely day hours. I'd slept over at Arden's house before, of course, but it had never felt like this, like I was just a shadow at the edge of their lives, like my own home was a million miles away instead of just down the road.

I put on my shoes and went out the front door as quiet as I could. The western horizon was still dark, the first rays of sun only just starting to peek up over the house behind me. The air around me was hot and heavy with raindrops that couldn't figure out how to fall.

I sat down on Arden's front step, where the concrete was still cool against my legs.

Fifteen days. It had only been fifteen days since that night I'd come in to find Mama in the kitchen cutting out watermelon seeds like her salvation depended on it. It had been hardly more than two weeks since all those small signs, those little out-of-place things that had come out of Mama's mouth since Mylie was born, had gotten impossible to ignore.

And in all that time, nothing I'd done had made a lick of difference.

A semitruck blew past on the highway, louder than the thunder, its own little windstorm roaring behind it—the only thing moving in that squashed-feeling morning.

I rubbed my face, just like Daddy did when he was feeling stressed, and let my head drop into my hands. The world pressed down on me, with the weight of the whole summer rolled up into one big crush.

Mama was sick, and nothing I or the doctors or anyone had done had fixed her. She'd gotten so bad she'd even lost sight of the fact that she wasn't normal. She'd up and got rid of her pills—the one thing that had ever made her regular, made her *real*, in my whole life.

I hadn't cried when Daddy had come to tell me the news yesterday morning. I hadn't cried since then, either. Distantly, I wondered if something was wrong with me. Who didn't cry when their own mama got taken up to the hospital in an ambulance?

There was a hard, dull ache underneath my rib cage, where my heart had gotten so chock-full of sadness and worry that it had grown a case around it, sharp and flinty.

Suddenly a spot on my arm burned needle-sharp, bad

enough that I jumped and shouted, not even remembering to stay quiet so I didn't wake up Arden's whole family inside the house. I clapped my hand to the sore place. It was already turning red. A fuzzy black-and-gold shape looped away from me, toward Miss Amanda's front garden.

"You stupid old bee!" I called after it, loud as I dared. "I hope you're the kind that's gonna go somewhere and die for what you did to me!"

I bit my lip hard, rubbing at the bee sting and wishing more than I had maybe in my whole life that my mama was there, and healthy, and able to wrap me up in her arms just the way Miss Amanda had done last night.

I tried, Mama, I thought, watching the place the bee had disappeared. *I tried so hard to make you better.*

I blinked again. I'd tried everything I knew—all except the one thing I'd been too scared to try.

I'd been so fixed on healing Mama's brain, I'd never been willing to go at things any other way. I'd been too afraid of the idea that Mama's sickness might be a part of our lives forever, too afraid that Miss Tabitha was right and that my stubborn heart was the thing that needed fixing, not Mama's brain.

Inside my chest, my heart in its hard shell thumped once, hard.

The bee. I kept rubbing at my arm, but the pain was quieter now, dissolving into the background of the idea that was taking hold of me like a summer thunderstorm.

There was something I needed to do before I saw Mama and Daddy again.

CHAPTER TWENTY-TWO

I kept glancing back at Arden's house as I walked down the driveway, but I couldn't see anybody stirring. The sun was still only just creeping up into the sky and flooding the road with silvery cloud-filtered light—and while people in Maryville got up early, I figured I had at least a few minutes to get out of sight. I hoped Arden would sleep in a bit, so that nobody had a chance to realize I was missing until I'd already made it where I needed to go.

I walked in the dry ditch bed beside the road, hardly noticing how the long weeds tickled at my bare shins. The heat was already rising up, radiating from the asphalt down over me, until I found myself wondering how on earth I still had water left to sweat out.

I'd only been to Miss Tabitha Quigley's house a few times, and not once since Grandpa and Grandma had moved out last year. With only three of us to manage a whole farm, there wasn't time for me to ride along with Mama when she went on easy errands like buying honey.

Still, I knew where it was just like I know where everything in Maryville is: not hard to do when there's not even enough people in town to fill up an elementary school. The Bee Lady's place was a mile or two north of us, a little white house tucked in between two farms with a shimmering view of the Albemarle Sound behind and a beehive sign that advertised *Honey and Other Products* for sale.

I judged I was about halfway there when my legs started threatening to fold up underneath me. It felt like days since I'd had a good sleep, days since I'd drunk enough water to replace all the sweat I was losing, days since I'd done anything that didn't leave me dizzy and tired. The rhythm of my steps pounded in my brain: *one-two-one-two-one-two.*

It almost sounded like *Mama, Mama, Mama.*

I was shaking when I finally came into sight of the little white house with the beehive sign out front. My arms trembled and my legs might have belonged to somebody else—they just kept going and going and going while the rest of me was begging them to stop.

But I couldn't stop. Not this close—not before I saw what Miss Tabitha thought she could offer me.

It was still pretty early, I guessed maybe almost breakfast time. Still, the door was unlocked, with a little sign that read *Come In* in cursive with a little bee on the end, like the bee had written the words out herself. When I opened the door, a bell above it jingled, *tink-tink*.

The room I stood in was filled with light, even on this gray cloud-lined morning, and had shelves on every wall filled with jars and jars of honey in every color from pale yellow to dark amber. On the floor below the shelves were huge two-gallon buckets with labels stamped on them: *COASTAL WILDFLOWER HONEY, COTTON BLOSSOM HONEY, BLACKBERRY HONEY*, and lots of others I couldn't read from where I stood.

There were other things on the shelves, too—fancy-shaped yellow bricks of beeswax, little displays of stacked-up lip balm containers, those plastic straws filled with honey that Grandma and Grandpa Kelly were always convinced counted as a real treat.

The house was quiet, the kind of quiet a house gets when you're the only living soul inside it, but through the window to the backyard I could see Miss Tabitha.

She was standing by one of the white beehive boxes, a sheet of honeycomb in her hands. A cloud of bees swirled around her, so many bees that the ends of her blond hair lifted in the wind they made. She wasn't wearing one of those white space suits beekeepers are supposed to put on to protect themselves from stings—but she didn't look afraid, not one bit. She looked more at home there, in that storm of bees, than she'd ever seemed in church or at the bank or the Duck-Thru Food Store.

I didn't tap on the window or even move, but after half a second she looked up and saw me, just like the bees had whispered to her that she had a guest. With a smile, she slid the honeycomb back into the bee box and walked toward the house. The bees parted for her like the ocean had parted for Moses in the Bible.

I swallowed hard.

"Why, Della Kelly," she said as she came through the back door. When I looked down at her white feet, they were bare, even though she had a pearl necklace strung around her neck and wore a long, flowing purple skirt. "You're here awful early. Most folks want Monday morning to drag on as late as possible. What can I get for you?"

The honey-lined shelves around me gave a little twist and spin, and I blinked hard. The Bee Lady moved forward, one hand reaching up toward me like she thought I was gonna fall right down on her waxed wood floor.

"Hold that thought. You can tell me what you've come for in a minute. You come on into my kitchen and sit yourself down before you collapse, shug. You look dog tired."

I nodded and followed her through a doorway and into the kitchen. It was like being inside a honeycomb: golden-yellow walls, that same wood floor that shone like honey, even a pale yellow refrigerator that looked old enough to have been in the Garden of Eden.

Miss Tabitha pulled a chair out from the table and waved at me to sit down, then scurried around the kitchen, pouring me a glass of lemonade and spreading butter and honey over a thick slice of bread.

"You eat and drink, now," she said, settling into the chair beside me with a glass of lemonade of her own, "and when you're feeling better, you can tell me what I can do for you. Sakes, child, where's your daddy? You're half-dead on your feet."

I sipped the lemonade—it was cool and tangy and tasted like the best thing that had ever hit my tongue— and tried to figure out how to answer. She didn't ask where Mama was, which meant she knew all about the ambulance coming yesterday, and the hospital. I expected most people did by now. News traveled fast in Maryville, and an ambulance was definitely *news*.

"My daddy had to stop by the church," I lied. "He, uh . . . wanted to get some notes from yesterday's sermon. To share with Mama. I just walked on over from there." It was less than a mile down the highway from the Bee Lady's house to the church. "I'm gonna meet him again when I'm done."

Miss Tabitha looked at me like she was trying to see down into my soul, her bright blue eyes sharp as lasers. I ate my bread and tried to act natural. I was pretty sure I remembered the hospital having its own Sunday sermon, last time Mama had been in there, but hopefully Miss Tabitha wouldn't know that.

Finally, she seemed to decide I was telling the truth, because she relaxed back into her chair and took a long drink of her own lemonade.

"My lands, it's hot out there this morning," she said, though she didn't seem to have a drop of sweat on her. I didn't answer, just shoveled in the rest of my bread. I was still hungry, but I didn't feel anymore like I was going to keel over right there in the Bee Lady's honey-colored kitchen.

I took a deep breath. "Miss Tabitha, you remember

I asked you two weeks ago if you had any honey that could heal my mama?" The Bee Lady nodded, eyes piercing again. "You said you didn't, but you said . . . you told me . . ."

I looked down, tracing a finger along the whorls of the wooden kitchen table.

"I told you I had something that could heal *you*, if you wanted it."

"Yeah. That."

"You think you're ready to give it a try, child?"

I nodded, one quick up-down of my chin, not trusting myself to say anything.

"You stay right here a quick minute while I go grab it." Miss Tabitha rose and swished back into the shop room, purple skirt swirling around her bare feet.

I finished up my lemonade, even crunching the ice cubes with my teeth and swallowing them down, their frozen coolness better than jumping into a swimming pool after my long, hot morning.

"Ah! Found it." A moment later Miss Tabitha popped back into view, a tiny yellow canning jar in her hand. She set it down on the table beside me. I reached a tentative finger out, touching the warm glass like a feather's kiss, almost afraid to breathe.

"This particular honey is a kind my bees have never

made before," Miss Tabitha went on. "And they didn't make much before they moved on to other flowers, back in the springtime. But while they were making it, they were single-minded, only ever visiting those blossoms. I figured if my bees felt it was important enough to make, it was important enough for me to keep separate from everything else—and when you stopped me at church that Sunday and asked for help, I just knew this was for you."

"What kind of honey is it?"

"Watermelon blossom. They paid lots of visits to your daddy's farm, and Mr. Hawthorne's, too."

My head shot up so fast my ponytail made a little breeze above my neck. The Bee Lady was quiet, her expression unreadable.

"And there's one other thing, Della. You have to understand that I don't always know the effects my honeys are gonna have. You see, their magic is that they bring out the strength a thing—or a person—has already got inside. Your grandpa's leg would've healed one way or another—my grandma's honey just sped that process up. All those other stories you've heard, all those Quigley honey miracles, they all came about because there was strength deep down inside those people, all along. It just took the honey to find it."

She tapped the lid of the honey jar with one white finger. "I think this honey will help you, Della, I really do. But it might take some time, and it might not be just in the way you expect it to. Sometimes, it takes patience to see what the honey's showing."

I nodded, only just now realizing I didn't have anything to pay her with. I knew the Bee Lady sold her honey cheaper to locals than the tourists who saw her sign and stopped on their way down to Plymouth, but cheap still wasn't the same as free.

"How much does it . . . um . . ."

"No cost this time, shug. Just think of it as me and the bees looking out for you."

I swallowed, picking the honey jar up in my hand. It was heavier than it looked; as I turned it, the honey slid slowly away from the side, almost seeming to glow in the kitchen light.

"Thanks, Miss Tabitha."

"You are most welcome, Della. I hope it gives you what you need."

I stood up and pushed my chair in toward the table. "I better get going to meet my daddy. Thanks for the snack, too."

"You take care of yourself, child. It's hot as sin out there today. I wish that rain would come on and put us all out of our misery." As if to punctuate her words, a thunderclap rattled the windows and made us both jump. Miss Tabitha laughed. "Maybe I oughta give you a ride down to the church, just in case it starts."

"No, ma'am," I said real fast. "I'll be okay. Besides, if it hasn't rained on us all summer, why would it start now?"

Miss Tabitha sighed. "Fair point, Della. Go quick and stay safe, then."

The shop bell tinkled again as I left, clicking the door shut behind me, the honey jar held tight in my hand.

The sky outside was darker than it had been when I'd gotten there, and the thunder was coming more often. The air was staticky, so that I almost expected my hair to stand up around my head the way it did when I jumped on Arden's trampoline. I shivered and started back down the highway.

I'd only been walking for a few minutes, the white siding of the Bee Lady's house just barely disappeared from view around a bend in the road, when a clap of thunder maybe louder than any I'd ever heard shook the ground below me and split the sky wide open.

A second later, the rain began.

CHAPTER TWENTY-THREE

I was wet as a drowned dog before I'd even had a chance to realize that it was finally, *finally* raining. The water sluiced down from the sky like God was pouring it from giant-size buckets, filling the ditch beside me so fast the water was higher every time I blinked. If it kept up this way, I'd only have ten or fifteen minutes before I'd have to hop right up onto the highway or be up to my ankles in brown running ditch water.

Had Arden and her mama and daddy noticed I was missing yet? Were they out there somewhere looking for me?

I clutched the jar of watermelon honey tighter and started walking again, hardly even able to see the road, my feet slip-sliding around on the wet rubber of my flip-flops. The rain was loud all around me, and lightning flashed again and again, followed quickly by thunder that boomed right through to my bones. You couldn't be a Carolina kid without learning to love summertime thunderstorms, and plenty of times Arden and I would run outside and dance around or jump in puddles, loving the feel of that warm rain on our skin.

This thunderstorm, though, was the kind we definitely wouldn't have been allowed out in. I bit my lip and walked faster, my head bent against the driving rain as thunder clapped again. Between sneaking out and getting caught in the kind of storm that put people into the newspaper with headlines like "Girl Struck by Lightning on Country Highway," I'd be in a world of hurt trying to explain myself to Miss Amanda when I got back to her place.

A blue car swooshed by me on the road, tires throwing up such a sheet of water I could feel it splatter against me even in the downpour. A second later the back lights blinked on, and before I knew it the car was turning around—not the easiest thing to do on a skinny highway like the kind we've got—and heading back toward me, slower now. My fingers gripped the honey jar so hard I thought it might break in my hand.

The car slowed to a stop and the driver's window hummed its way down.

"Good heavens, child, what on earth are you doing out here in this storm?"

It was Miss Lorena Bradley, her sunshine smile so kind and friendly that before I knew it something big and rough had broken loose inside me and my chin was trembling hard, just one breath away from tears.

"Never mind you telling me that," Miss Lorena said, waving me closer. "You just get on in here with me and we'll figure out what to do with you, all right?" She reached for a button, and I heard the doors unlock.

"I'll get your seats all wet."

"Seats dry lots easier than little girls."

Taking a deep breath, I climbed in next to her.

"I been looking for you everywhere," Miss Lorena said, glancing over at me. "Driving up and down this highway the last half hour. Mr. Hawthorne's doing the same thing, down south. Only reason I knew to come this way again was because Amanda Hawthorne got a call from your daddy up in Alberta, who'd gotten a call from Tabitha Quigley, all in a panic about how she'd let you walk out of her place just before the rain started, and you'd been gone before she could catch up with you to tell you to come on back inside."

I twisted guiltily in the seat. "Didn't mean to make anyone worry." Least of all the whole bee-stung town.

"I know, sugar. I'll get you back to their house right quick, and everything will be just fine."

"I can't go back there," I said before I could stop myself. The wind-and-thunder feeling of last night's fight with Arden was thick around me, and I wasn't sure if it would be harder showing my face to her or to Miss Amanda after running away this morning.

Miss Lorena was silent for a minute, the only sound the *whoosh* of the car's tires on the wet road and the rain coming down all around us.

"I'll tell you what," she said finally. "I'm going to send Arden's mama a text to say I got you. I need to make a quick stop by my own house so Thomas has got the study book he left in here, and then you can fill me in on what's going on and we'll figure out what to do with you."

"Okay," I whispered, trying to keep the tears back.

We rode without talking, Miss Lorena humming a hymn under her breath until we pulled into the long cement driveway that wound behind the gas station and out to Mr. Anton's house. Mr. Anton waved as we passed by the gas station; he was outside changing the buckets of soapy water he kept by the pumps for drivers to wash off their windshields.

"Sit tight and I won't be a minute," Miss Lorena said, popping out of the car and closing the door behind her. The rain was finally starting to ease up, coming down in something more like a whisper than a roar as she hurried down the driveway toward the house.

I looked back down at the honey jar, warm in my hands, almost glowing in the gloom of the storm. Biting my lip, I unscrewed the jar and dipped my finger in, bringing the honey up to my mouth and licking it off.

Please, God, let this fix everything, I thought.

The honey was an explosion of sweet on my tongue, thick and full of sunlight and fruit and something else wild and strange that wasn't like any honey I'd ever tasted before. I closed my eyes, sucking it all off my finger, my heart singing, *Let it work, let it work, let it work.*

I ate some more honey, watching the rain come down out the windows and trying not to think too much. Why on earth had I followed up the bad idea of running away with the even *worse* idea of doing it again? Would Miss Amanda ever forgive me? Did Daddy know what I'd done?

Somehow, here in Miss Lorena's car with the rain pattering down on the roof above me, the honey in my little jar seemed much less magical than it had when I'd been sitting in the Bee Lady's kitchen. How in blazes was honey supposed to fix anything at all, when things were this broken?

And, said a tiny voice in the back of my mind that I couldn't shut up even though I didn't want to listen, *when I broke them in the first place?*

The sound of a tap on my window made me jump. Thomas stood outside it, his bronze skin shining with rainwater and a smile on his face. I rolled it down and he poked his head in.

"Mama said you were waiting out here. Thought I'd come say hi. I heard a rumor you'd run away."

My cheeks burned red.

"Anyway, I'm glad you're back," Thomas went on. "I meant what I said before about getting you to tutor me sometime. I still can't make heads or tails of algebra. And somebody's going to need to be around to help Mylie when she gets bigger, too. Skill with numbers is hard to come by. Plus, things around your place were a lot quieter with you gone. I thought your daddy was gonna up and forget how to talk."

I blushed even deeper, but couldn't help my lips twitching up into a little smile, either.

"Oh, and I've got something for you, too, Della. I nearly forgot." Thomas put a little blue paperback book through the window and onto my lap. It was called *The Graveyard Book*, and on the front there was a strange-looking tombstone and a shiny gold medal.

"It's one of my favorites," he said. "I read it a lot last year, after my daddy—well." He shrugged. "It's kind of different. It's all about families, though, families that don't always look regular. I figured you might need something like that yourself right now."

"Thanks," I said, tracing the medal.

"No problem. It's yours as long as you want to keep it. See ya," he said, waving as he ducked back out of the car, before he turned to jog down the driveway toward the house again.

His minute-long visit had added something different to the jumble of feelings inside of me: swirling through the worry and the sadness and the knotting in my insides was a tiny springtime bloom, like the finger-long purple crocuses that popped up all around our front porch step in February, before the sun had even come back into the sky.

CHAPTER TWENTY-FOUR

I'd eaten a lot more of the honey by the time Miss Lorena came back, spooning it into my mouth with my finger and not even bothering to savor it anymore. My stomach was starting to feel strange, a little bit achy and a little bit floaty, and I still wasn't any closer to knowing what to do about Mama.

"The honey brings out the strength that's already there," Miss Tabitha had said when she'd handed it to me.

But what if there wasn't any strength in me to be brought out at all?

"Okay," said Miss Lorena, hopping back into the driver's seat and then turning around to look at me, her dark eyes touched all through with gold. "Now, Miss Della, you fill me in."

All the crocus happiness that Thomas had carried with him earlier sucked out of me so fast it made me dizzy. I opened my mouth but couldn't get any words past the thickness in my throat.

"Oh, sweet girl," said Miss Lorena, "you just take your time. We can sit in this old driveway as long as you need. What's going on?"

This time the tears came on slow but strong, until my whole body was shaking with sobs like the thunder that still echoed, far away where the sky dipped down to kiss the earth. Miss Lorena reached over and stroked my hair, her fingers like butterfly wings.

"That's right," she murmured, so soft I could hardly hear it over my own crying. "You just get it all out, honey. You just get it all out."

Finally the sobs slackened and the tears quieted down. The hole inside me, though, felt bigger than ever, dark and gaping, so that it hurt to breathe in.

"It's my fault," I blurted, scrubbing at my eyes with the back of my hand. I'd never said those words, not ever—not even to Arden. Not even whispered in the middle of the hard nights to Mylie where she slept in her crib. Somehow, it felt easier to say them to Miss Lorena, who was so new here; maybe if I said it to this kind stranger with her smile like June, she wouldn't hate me as much as I knew my own parents would.

"What's your fault, baby?"

"It's my fault that Mama's sick." I stared down at the carpeting on the floor of the car, kicked at a loose loop of polyester with my toe. "And it's my fault she had to go to the hospital."

"How do you figure that, hmm?"

"She was just fine until I came along. The schizophrenia didn't come on until I was born. Dr. DuBose says it was triggered by the hormones and the stress. And—" I took a deep, shaky breath. "I ran away, didn't I? I didn't even stick around to help my own mama. If I had stayed . . . maybe she wouldn't have gotten so bad."

"Oh, sweetheart." Miss Lorena's hand kept moving on the back of my head. I wanted to lean into it, wanted to let that feeling be all I paid attention to, but I couldn't. "You listen to me, sweet Della. There is nothing you did that caused your mama's problems, and nothing that you could have done to change it, you hear me? A thing like schizophrenia is bigger than you, bigger than me, bigger than your mama and daddy. It's a sickness, just as real as anything like cancer, and it needs a doctor's help just as much.

"And one way or another, that sickness would have found your mama eventually, honey. You being born was one trigger, but if that hadn't happened, something else would have. And the same with this weekend. Your mama's been up against a lot this year, as I understand it. And that little sister of yours is a pistol. It's not anything you did, or didn't do, I promise."

"You really think so?"

"I know so."

"I just . . . I just wanted her to be a normal mama. I just wanted to be a normal kid. Not all this"—I swallowed, squeezing my honey jar—"worrying."

"I know, honey. I know you do. And I'll tell you straight, Della—probably, your mama is never going to be quite like other mothers out there. My guess is she's always going to have to struggle with this, and that'll be a struggle for you and your daddy and Mylie, too. Everybody's got burdens, honey, and this is the burden that belongs to *your* family. But I also know that if your mama had to trade you and your sister in for being perfectly healthy, she wouldn't do it."

"How do you know that?"

Miss Lorena smiled. "Because I'm a mama, too." She put her hand on her chest. "And once you have a child, it's like a part of your heart is out there walking around in the world, and it's the biggest blessing you could possibly imagine."

I put my own hand to my chest, feeling the way my

heart tapped against my ribs, trying to picture what that might feel like.

"There's something else, too," I added after a minute.

"What's that?"

I squeezed my fingers into fists. Deep inside my heart, deeper even than the fear that Mama would never get better and that it was my fault she was sick in the first place, another fear was nestled, hard and sharp and thick.

"If it happened to Mama . . . could it happen to me one day, too, do you think? Someday when I grow up and want to have babies?"

"Oh, honey." Miss Lorena was still as still, and when she spoke again, I could see that her eyes were shining and wet. "I guess none of us really know, do we? None of us ever know what seeds of pain are living inside us, waiting to sprout sometime in the future. You remember how I told you about Thomas's daddy—how he had cancer in his family, how his own daddy died of it?"

I nodded.

"It's something we talked about a lot, him and me, when we were dating. About how that cancer could be lurking inside him, ready to spring out and change all our lives forever. And then one day—it did."

"But—" I stopped, sniffling. "Wasn't it hard, marrying

him and knowing that might come for you someday?"

"Sure it was. But that's life. You just gotta take it a day at a time, honey. You might have to live with this fear inside you for a long time. And it might be hard. But you'll make it through—I know you will. You're tough, Miss Della Kelly. I could tell that the moment I met you."

I gave a watery little smile.

"And one more thing I need you to know, Della. If things ever get too much to handle for you at your house, you know you're always welcome to come on over and see me. And I know that Mrs. Hawthorne feels just the same way, and I bet plenty of other mamas in this town do, too."

"Thanks," I whispered.

"Tell me," said Miss Lorena, pulling her purse up from the floor onto her lap. "Last week when you brought me back Emily Dickinson's poems. Did you do that because you thought you needed to be taking care of your mama and not reading?"

I nodded, the memory of the day I'd been reading by the chicken coop rising up until I could hardly breathe.

She reached into her bag and pulled out the little blue book, that smile creeping back onto her face. "I thought that might be it. I want you to have this, honey. Not just from the little library, either, but as a gift."

My hand reached out without me even telling it to, running a finger across the soft blue cover.

"Go on, take it."

"You sure?"

Miss Lorena nodded, pushing the book forward until it was in my hands instead of hers. I laid it on my lap on top of the book Thomas had brought me earlier. Seemed to me the Bradleys mostly knew how to talk through books.

"Sometimes when things are bad for me, books get to be some of my best friends," Miss Lorena said, smiling like she could read my thoughts. "Maybe this one can be yours. Now, I can take you back to Arden's if you want, but while I was inside I spoke with Mrs. Hawthorne on the phone, and I'm thinking it might be even better if you let me take you to the hospital to see your parents. I know it would mean the world to your mama. It'll be awhile before visiting hours start, but we can go up and find your daddy, get you some lunch."

"I'm scared," I said, pulling the books to my chest and hugging them, like armor. "I don't want to see her . . . like that."

"But it's something you're gonna have to do at some point, child. Might as well be now."

I nodded and swallowed again, lowering the books down to my lap and flipping through the pages of the *POEMS*, not saying anything else as Miss Lorena pulled her seat belt on and put the car into gear.

As we got back on the highway, the tapping of the rain and the swooshing of the tires on the wet road was like a heartbeat, or the ocean, rushing in and out of my ears and making my own nervous heart beat a little slower. I read through a few of Emily Dickinson's poems, still not understanding most of them but liking the way they sounded in my head, trying to think of anything except where we were going.

A few pages in there was one that made me stop and read it through twice.

> *Hope is the thing with feathers*
> *That perches in the soul,*
> *And sings the tune without the words,*
> *And never stops at all . . .*

I looked up from the book, at the rain-washed window and the gray sky outside. "What am I gonna say to Mama when I see her?" I whispered.

Miss Lorena kept her eyes on the road, but her voice was as warm and sweet as the taste of the Bee Lady's honey, as kind as if she'd wrapped her arms around me the way Miss Amanda had the night before. "Oh, sugar. You don't have to say anything at all, if you don't want to. You just being there will be like a gift to your mama. I promise you that."

"Okay," I said, leaning against the door beside me, trying my hardest to feel that thing with feathers fluttering inside my soul.

CHAPTER TWENTY-FIVE

Sometimes in the detective shows I watched with Daddy, they'd have a scene inside a hospital room—somebody lying in a bed with white sheets and a whole panel of buttons to make it move, surrounded by beeping machines and doctors who talked in some kind of doctor code.

Mama's hospital wasn't anything like that.

After Miss Lorena had dropped me off at Grandma and Grandpa's in time to have lunch and catch a little nap on their guest bed—I'd been so tired I could hardly keep my eyes open by that point—Daddy had left Mylie with Grandma and Grandpa and brought me here, to the hospital. We'd checked in at the front desk and found the unit where Mama was staying, guarded by locked double doors so big and heavy that looking at them sent a crawling spider of a shiver down my spine.

Those doors seemed to be saying, *We've got her, and we aren't letting her go anytime soon*, and I felt the hot press of tears in the back of my throat again.

There was a loud click when the doors unlocked to let us through. I slid my hand into Daddy's, like I was Mylie's age again, too afraid to walk through into that strange place without being able to feel another person's pulse up against my own.

We followed a nurse through the doorway and into a great big room with green walls and bookshelves and so much light pouring in from the windows that it was like the sun itself had decided to pay the hospital a visit. The rain had finished and the clouds outside had pulled apart to let the sun peek through and make a rainbow, a tiny little sky-gift that made me stand my shoulders up straighter.

"Della, baby, your mama may not seem quite like her normal self," Daddy murmured, rubbing at his forehead with his free hand. He was tired and pale, with big dark circles under his eyes and the front part of his hair sticking up, like he hadn't brushed it or looked in a mirror for days.

I nodded, looking again at that little wisp of rainbow, at all the sunlight caught up in that room, holding my honey jar tight and wishing I'd eaten just a little bit more.

The nurse stopped at a door right off the sunlight room. Next to the door was a whole wall of windows that showed a long, narrow place almost like a cafeteria, except that there was no food—little square tables surrounded with armless chairs covered in an abstract green-and-gray-patterned fabric.

The room was empty.

"Y'all go on and wait in here," the nurse said, waving us inside. She had dusky skin and an accent you could wrap yourself up in, so that *here* sounded like it had three syllables. "Wherever you like. I'll go get Suzanne."

Daddy and I sat at the closest table. I clenched my hands together so hard they hurt.

After a minute, the door opened again, and Mama walked in.

"Oh, Della, baby," she said, tears squeezing out of her eyes and running down her cheeks, and somehow the warm sweetness of her words slid right inside me, wrapping my heart in their sound until I could feel the tickle of that thing with feathers perched in my soul.

"I'm so glad to see you," Mama went on, talking

fast, like she was afraid she wouldn't say everything she needed to in time. "I was so worried about you, honey, so worried that they were going to hurt you. I looked and looked for you but couldn't find where they took you."

The flutter inside me stopped abruptly, like that little hope bird had been smothered. I squeezed my honey jar. "Nobody took me, Mama. I went to Arden's by myself."

Mama was talking again before I even finished. "No, no, I know there's people trying to hurt you, hurt Mylie, too. I couldn't keep you safe, honey, so I had to do my best with Mylie." Her tears were coming faster now; the nurse stepped forward, putting a hand on Mama's shoulder. She had a silver ring with a big diamond that caught the light, sending little sparkles of color all around the room.

Just like that rainbow outside the window.

Your mama is never going to be quite like other mothers out there, Miss Lorena had said earlier. I'd tried everything I knew, every idea I'd had and then some, and none of it had fixed Mama's crazy.

No, I thought, remembering how much Daddy hated it when I called Mama crazy, remembering how Mama had winced once when she'd heard a man at church refer to people like her that way.

Not crazy. Sick.

I swallowed. Before Miss Lorena had left Grandma and Grandpa's, she'd given me another hug and whispered, *You just remember what I told you, sugar. You just remember that you can always come to me if you need me.* And as I'd watched the front door swing closed after her, I could have sworn I'd tasted the wild sweetness of the Bee Lady's honey on my tongue again, like a tiny piece of sunlight washing all the way through my storm.

But right now there was nothing, just the dry, sour taste of my own nervousness.

The nurse was rubbing Mama's shoulder back and forth. "Calm down, Suzanne honey," she said in a low voice like the rocking of a boat on the sound. "Your babies are just fine. They got good people taking care of them, just like we taking care of you." But Mama's tears kept on coming, with her not even bothering to wipe them, just looking at me like she was drowning and I was the rope.

I took a deep breath. "I love you, Mama," I said, wishing the Bee Lady were there in the room with us so I could yell and cry and throw her honey jar back in her face. It hadn't fixed Mama and it hadn't fixed me, either; standing here listening to her saying awful things and not even realizing it was just as bad as ever. Miss

Tabitha may have thought there was strength in me for that honey to find, but she was wrong.

There was no fluttering thing with feathers in my chest now, just a hot burn of pain that went right through to my heart.

"She's doing better than she was when they brought her in yesterday," the nurse said to Daddy and me, "but it's gone take a day or two for the medications they gave her to really start doing their job. I'm sorry, but I think y'all had better go so we can get her something to help her calm down a bit."

Daddy nodded, rubbing his forehead again, a whole galaxy of sadness inside his eyes. He leaned forward and set a kiss on Mama's forehead, wiping a tear off her cheek with his big dirt-stained hand. "You get better fast and come back to us, Suzanne. It's not home without you, sweetheart."

I hugged Mama, trying not to feel how trembly and frail she seemed, about to float away on the breeze any minute. Nothing at all like the mama who could make me laugh on bad days and keep all the storms in the world from reaching me. I blinked my eyes hard, wishing that it was Miss Amanda or Miss Lorena here with me now and not the mama who seemed less and less like a real mother by the day. She was talking fast again, big strings of words that didn't have anything to do with each other and were impossible to understand.

"We'll see you tomorrow, Mr. Kelly," the smiley nurse said, ushering me and Daddy out of the visiting room and back through the heavy double doors faster than I could so much as catch my breath.

The doors locked behind us as we stepped into the elevator, the click like a crack of thunder that rang in my ears all the long way down.

"Della," said Daddy as I slid into the passenger seat of his truck, trying not to look back at the hospital. He turned the key in the ignition and the truck rumbled to life, but he just sat there with his hands on the steering wheel, not taking off the parking brake. "I want to tell you that I'm sorry for making you feel I'd let you down, with your mama and her pills."

He breathed—*in, out*—and I could have sworn I'd seen a glimmer of something bright in his eyes.

"When you disappeared, I felt terrible, honey, most especially because I knew it was my fault. The last couple weeks have been hard on all of us, probably you more than anyone. I know I put too much on you, Della. More than any twelve-year-old girl should have to carry. I'm so sorry."

I looked down at my hands, curled around the honey jar and the books Thomas and Miss Lorena had given me. "Wasn't there anything you could've done?" I asked, the words bitter and sharp on my tongue. Tears were brimming in my eyes again, spilling hot and wet onto my cheeks.

"I don't know, baby," Daddy said, his fingers tight on the steering wheel. "I don't know."

"I just—" I paused, scrubbing at my eyes. "Won't she ever get better?"

I thought I'd done all my crying earlier that afternoon with Miss Lorena, but I was wrong. The cab of the truck around me swam in swirls of color and light.

"I don't know, baby girl. She'll get better than she is right now, sure, but I can't promise it won't ever happen again. This is her cross to bear, and all of ours, too, and it's something none of us caused and none of us can change."

"Daddy—" I closed my eyes. "How come you and Mama decided to get pregnant with Mylie, when you knew it was me being born that made her get sick in the first place?"

"It didn't *make* her get sick, honey. The schizophrenia was always going to be a part of her. If it hadn't been after you were born, it would've shown up some other time."

"Okay, but still. Why did you decide to have another baby when Mama got so sick after me? Wasn't I enough?"

"Oh, Della." Daddy turned around and looked at me, his eyes full up with so much love I almost couldn't breathe, and not from the crying this time. "Sweetheart, your mama and I love you so much—that's exactly *why* we wanted Mylie. We just couldn't abide the thought of going all through life without another little girl or boy to love, too. And we knew what we were doing, I promise. Dr. DuBose worked with us every step of your mama's pregnancy—you know that. We knew it might be tough, but we also knew it would be worth it."

"I just want Mama to come back to us—to her *real* self."

Daddy turned to the wheel again, putting down the emergency brake and backing out of the parking space with a loud engine-revving noise.

"Me too, Della. I do, too."

CHAPTER TWENTY-SIX

We slept that night at Grandma and Grandpa's house a few minutes from the hospital, me and Daddy and Mylie all crowded into Grandma and Grandpa's guest room. Daddy snored on and on, and Mylie kept waking up and crying for Mama.

A little while after the numbers on the digital clock on the dresser had passed midnight and started back at one, I heard the rain start up again outside—soft and steady this time, a gentle patter-patter-drip on the roof.

When I finally fell asleep, lying on the floor next to Mylie in her Pack 'n Play, I dreamed I was back at the hospital, holding on to that rainbow for dear life while Mama talked in riddles and my honey jar fell to the ground, smashed into glittering pieces.

The next morning I woke up feeling washed-out and tired, like all those tears I'd cried yesterday and the day before had taken the snap out of me somehow.

When nobody was looking, I pulled out my honey jar and drizzled golden honey over my plate of cheese grits at breakfast, and swirled some into my cup of sweet tea just to be thorough. Everyone was too busy telling Mylie to stop throwing all her food onto the ground to pay attention to me.

"Sweetheart, I think it would be best if I visited Mama alone this afternoon," said Daddy to me after we'd gotten the breakfast dishes all cleared away. "I know she's gonna want you to come plenty while she's there, but for the next few days she's going to need a lot of rest and quiet, while Dr. DuBose tries to get her medications sorted out and working for her."

I stared straight ahead, putting my breakfast plate into the dishwasher. I didn't know whether I was more upset or more relieved. Seeing Mama yesterday hadn't been anything like I'd expected it to be, and it had spooked me more than I cared to admit.

Daddy sighed. "It's going to be tough for all of us while Mama's in the hospital, but we'll find a way to make it work. We're going to need to head home here in a few more minutes so I can get the farm chores done before visiting hours start, especially since I stayed up here and didn't get to them yesterday."

Grandma and Grandpa came to the door with us when we were ready to leave. Grandma hugged Daddy and Grandpa slapped him on the back, like men do when they don't feel like hugging.

"Next time, fill us in before Suzie ends up in the hospital," Grandpa said gruffly.

Daddy paused with his hand on the doorknob, guilt all over his face. "I know I should have told y'all sooner. I just—it's just been a tough summer, with Suzie's health and the drought and the farm, and I didn't want you to worry."

"Too late, son. I been worrying since we moved out. It's a lot of work for one man to handle all by himself."

Daddy shrugged. "It is what it is. I know you would've stayed till you were in your grave if you'd had your choice. But I've got a boy to help a few days a week now. We'll get by."

He bent and picked Mylie up and ran with her out into the rain.

"You take care of yourself, Della," Grandma said, pulling me in for a big hug. Her wrinkled white skin was soft and warm and smelled like the bread she'd made that morning. "And listen, watermelon girl, you call me if you need *anything*, you hear me? Your grandpa and I aren't living on the moon. Even if you just need to talk, sweetheart, you give me a call. I love you a bushel and a peck."

I nodded and followed Daddy out into the truck. Grandma and Grandpa stood at the door and waved until we'd lost sight of the house. I unscrewed the top of my honey jar and dipped my finger in—more out of habit, now, than because I actually thought it would do anything. I held the honey in my mouth and closed my eyes, wishing that Mama would be there at the end of the road to welcome us back home and recite poems to Mylie and scold me for not doing my chores quick enough.

I'd started out hoping I could fix everything wrong with Mama and help her remember how to mother us properly . . . and now here I was, with less of a mama than ever.

Except, I realized as the honey spread over my tongue, that wasn't the whole truth. I thought of Grandma's arms around me a few minutes ago, the way her eyes had brightened up when Daddy and I had walked through her front door yesterday afternoon.

And I thought of Miss Lorena hugging me yesterday, telling me twice that if things got too hard to handle at my home, I could come right on over to hers.

And Miss Amanda Sunday morning, wrapping her arms around me like I was her very own little girl. Miss Amanda, who'd been there for my whole life—all my birthday parties, all my growth spurts, the time I'd fallen off the front steps and knocked out my two front teeth when I was seven.

The brightness of the honey was moving on down through me now, filling up every bit of me with lightness and gold, so that when I looked down, the tips of my fingers glowed like candles with warm honey-colored light.

It's going to be okay, that glow was whispering all through me, waking up the little hope-bird in my chest again.

It was going to be okay, because even if I didn't have my own mama right now, I had a life—and a town—full of other mamas who were looking out for me. Some who were my own relations, like Grandma. Some who I'd known long enough they might as well be, like Miss Amanda. And some, like Miss Lorena, who I'd barely known for any time at all, but who still knew how to talk straight when I needed it and sing a song to that little fluttering thing in my soul.

And all those mamas, and probably some I hadn't

even noticed yet—they'd be watching over me, right there whenever I needed them, waiting for the time when my own mama was ready to step back into being the mother I needed her to be.

And my daddy, too. My daddy, who loved me and Mylie and Mama so much we were his whole world. My daddy, who took care of us all, who may not have been perfect but was sure trying hard. For the first time in weeks, I felt my heart softening up a bit, the anger and frustration at Daddy that I'd been holding to with tight fists unclenching a little. Just like me, Daddy had been doing the best he knew how.

And soon, Mama would be back home. And she would have her ups and her downs, but she would get through them. *We* would get through them, together. Because I knew, with all the lightness of that glow that radiated through me, that Mama loved me more than life itself. Even in her sickness, even when the edges of reality had started to tangle up around her, it had been me and Mylie she was worried for, me and Mylie she'd been trying to protect.

No sickness in the world could make my mama's love for us less real.

And none of us had to get through any of it on our own. Maybe, I thought suddenly, the Bee Lady's honey had known all along I didn't have enough strength inside of me to get through this all on my own.

Maybe what it was doing, right this very minute, was showing me that that was okay—that there was strength all around me, lifting me up when I needed it, stepping in when Mama and I both needed a little extra help.

And all those worries about the future that I'd confessed to Miss Lorena, about whether or not I'd end up like Mama—they'd still be there. They might not ever really go away. But I knew, deep down where the honey was sliding into my stomach like warm sunshine, that I'd be able to get through it either way.

In the car seat next to me, Mylie started squirming and whimpering that her seat belt was too tight and she wanted Mama. I reached my hand over and wrapped her chubby fingers around my thumb, *shhh*-ing until she calmed back down again.

"It's all right, little monster," I whispered, so soft I couldn't tell if she'd even heard me over the drum of the rain on the truck roof. "It's all right. Everything is gonna be just fine."

And right at that very moment, a little shaft of sunlight peeked through one of the gray rain clouds that was hiding it, and the whole sky turned as gold as the honey glow running through my veins.

CHAPTER TWENTY-SEVEN

It rained all that week and into the beginning of the next one, rain that sighed and cried until all the grass in Maryville started to turn green again, and on Sunday the preacher got up at the pulpit and gave thanks in a voice that trembled and dipped like the rain itself.

Every day Daddy drove his tractor through the mud puddles, and every day Mylie and I went out in the rain and picked as much as we could from the garden for Arden and Eli to sell at the farm stand. At first I'd taken Mylie with me and met Arden at the stand like normal, but it was near impossible to stop Mylie biting every single peach out there, and nobody wants peaches with great big old tooth marks in them. Plus, without Mama there, Daddy needed me more on the farm, helping him and Thomas pull weeds and pick squash beetles and harvest the first of the summer sweet corn.

The first time I'd seen Arden, the day after I'd gone to visit Mama in the hospital, neither of us had quite known what to say. We'd both hung back for a few minutes, like we hadn't known each other our whole lives, like maybe the things we'd whispered to each other in Arden's dark bedroom two nights ago had been too big to get past.

But then Arden had rushed up and closed the distance between us, and before I could even blink, her arms were around my neck. She'd smelled like peaches and nail polish and like the special, shiny kind of magic that the two of us made when we were together. When a pair of lucky ladybugs landed right there on the place where her arm met mine, I didn't even bother to brush them off.

And just like that, I'd known that there wasn't anything we could have said that could have broken up our friendship. It was strong and bright, like the boards Daddy and Mr. Ben went out to buy later that afternoon.

"What's that for?" I asked when they got back from the hardware store, Daddy's pickup full of two-by-fours.

"You'll see," Daddy said with the kind of smile I hadn't seen on his face in months and months. "You and Arden hop in the truck bed and come on out back with us. There's something we need your help with, down at the bay."

When we got down to the water, Daddy stepped out of the truck and started laying a tarp on the muddy ground.

"We're going to help you out and do some supervising," said Mr. Ben, jumping out the passenger side of the cab, "and you're going to need to use some real plans this time. But we figured you girls oughta have another playhouse."

"We're going to build it in the rain?" Arden asked.

Mr. Ben laughed. "No. We'll wait. We'll wrap the wood up good in the tarp and leave it out here for a nice day to hit. But we needed to go into town today anyway and figured we might as well get the lumber while we were at it, and let you girls in on the secret."

"Thanks, Dad!" Arden said, running to Mr. Ben and throwing her arms around his waist.

I couldn't say anything, standing there in the rain with my sandals sinking into the mud and my throat burning with something that felt an awful lot like tears.

But Daddy looked up and saw my face, and by the

way he smiled, I knew he could tell what I was thinking, anyway.

Daddy took a whole day after we got back from Grandma and Grandpa's to pull up the watermelon plants he hadn't been able to save, and sprayed the rest with the stuff Mr. Ben had given him to keep them all safe from the fungus.

"Probably won't be many to sell this summer," he said, "but we'll still have enough for us."

When he brought a melon in that night, I closed my eyes and bit into one of the ruby-red slices, letting the crisp cold flavor explode onto my tongue, and even though I couldn't stop myself from thinking of Mama and the way watermelon seeds had been the first clue that something wasn't right with her, it was okay. I was learning how to tuck those thoughts away in my heart and remind myself that she was getting better, and that we were all gonna get through it one way or another.

Because she *was* getting better—slowly, but truly. Every afternoon, Daddy drove up to Alberta and stayed with her for as long as he could before visiting hours ended or Mama got too upset.

All that first week she wasn't ready to see me again, though, and Daddy explained that it was because no matter how hard Mama tried, she couldn't shake the things her sickness whispered to her, the belief that me and Mylie were in danger, that she had to protect us from the whole world.

But Daddy said that every day he went up to the hospital, Mama had been calmer, had been able to stay longer in her own right mind.

And then, one week and two days after that thunderstorm day when Daddy had come to tell me that Mama'd been taken in an ambulance up to Alberta, he found me where I was working in the garden and told me that Mama wanted me to come up and visit that afternoon.

"It might not be for very long," he said, and I could tell he was nervous by the way his smile looked like somebody was jabbing him in the leg with a pin. "Your mama still has a ways to go before she's back to her usual self, but she's feeling lots better, and Dr. DuBose thinks they might have hit on the right med combination." The doctors had figured out pretty quickly that Mama's old pill wasn't working anymore, hadn't been working well enough since Mylie was born. So they'd decided to try some new ones, and maybe two together to get her sickness under her control as much as possible.

I picked some more bush beans, thinking I probably

looked like I'd been poked with a pin, too.

"You don't have to come if you don't want to," Daddy said quickly. "I know last week was hard."

"No," I said, putting a last handful of long green beans into my bucket. "I think . . . I do want to go."

We left Mylie at the Hawthornes' that afternoon. Miss Amanda gave me an extra-long hug before we left and pushed a bag with two fresh blackberry scones into my hand. I think that was her way of saying *I love you.*

"Everything is going to be just fine, Della," she whispered before she let go. "I know it is."

Daddy and I were silent all the way to the hospital, both of us busy listening to the rain drumming on the car and our own thoughts. My stomach was twisting worse than the roots of the weeds I'd spent the morning pulling out of the garden.

The lady at the front desk of the behavioral health building smiled and said, "Hey there, Miles," when we walked in, and by the time we stepped out of the elevator and onto Mama's floor, the heavy double doors were already unlocking and opening.

"Wait," I said. I couldn't make my feet take another step toward that room, toward the woman who might be the mama I knew or might be a stranger.

I closed my eyes, trying to summon up the way the

Bee Lady's watermelon honey had glowed all the way through me. I'd finished off every last lick of honey in the jar days ago, but I could still remember its wild brightness without even trying.

I didn't know what Mama would be like today, or when she'd be back to herself and ready to come home. It might be that today's visit would go great—or it could be just like last week, and I'd leave with Mama crying and saying things that only made sense in her own brain.

And it might be that someday I'd be like Mama, too, struggling to figure out what was real and what wasn't, never quite like the other mothers in town.

But I thought of Miss Amanda whispering that everything was going to be just fine. And somehow, I knew she was right.

Maybe it wouldn't be easy, but one way or another, all those things would work themselves out.

I opened my eyes. "Okay," I said, taking a deep in-out breath and looking down at my fingertips, which still held just the tiniest glimmer of candlelight. "I'm ready."

And we stepped through the doors.

ACKNOWLEDGMENTS

I had been writing for a long time before I learned just how many people it takes to create a book—and I think it's no coincidence that it wasn't until I'd managed to assemble an A-plus support team that *Where the Watermelons Grow* found a home.

First, this book would never have been what it is without the help and generosity of friends who were willing to answer my questions, read early drafts, and brainstorm with me as I worked to get the portrayal of Suzanne's situation as accurate as possible. Lisa Hyde, Tracey Enerson Wood, J. R. Yates, and Priscilla Mizell, thank you! Any errors in representation are mine alone.

I couldn't have written a word without the unflagging love of Shannon Cooley, who has always been there to cheer me on and cheer me up when I'm convinced I'm a talentless hack.

Amanda Rawson Hill, Jamie Pacton, and Ashley Martin: thank you, my beautiful Sisters of the Pen, for your pep talks, your brainstorming, your critiques, and your presence in my life. The three of you are shining examples of generosity and grace, and I'm blessed to call you friends.

The Pitch Wars community (especially my fellow 2015 alumni!) has been a game changer for my writing, and I'll never be able to express my gratitude enough. Among others, I'll always owe gratitude to Rosalyn Eves, who taught me what revision actually looks like, and to Julie Artz, Cory Leonardo, and Kit Rosewater for their friendship, love, and belief in me. Likewise, this book may never have found an agent and editor to love it without #DVPit and its tireless creator, Beth Phelan; I'm also grateful for the DVSquad, with whom I'll always feel like the shy, starstruck girl in the cafeteria tagging along with all the popular kids.

The Electric 18s and Class of 2k18 debut groups were my cheering section, my moral support, and my comic relief on the days I needed it most. The Storymakers writing community—especially my Sisters in Writing and Suite Sisters—have been there for me since the days when I was an overly cocky newbie with big dreams.

There are many critique partners who read various drafts of this book and helped make it stronger than I ever could've on my own. Particular thanks to Emily Ungar and Anna Carew-Miller, who helped suggest some of the final puzzle pieces as I revised. (What would this book even be without the Bee Stories?!)

I owe deep gratitude to Heather Clark, who heard me struggling with the early outline of this story in a workshop and came up with the perfect solution to my problem.

My family has written the book on supportiveness—especially my dad, Russ Ray, who has been my number one cheerleader for as long as I can remember. My mom has always been in my corner and has raised me to know just how important a mama's love is. My siblings taught me what it is to be the oldest in a family and how you can love a little brother or sister just as much as if they were your own child.

Though they may not be family by blood, I never would've had the courage to pursue writing as a career if not for the encouragement of Gwen Rasmussen and Sara Hagmann.

My life has been filled with women who have mothered me along with my own mama. Chief among them is Alisyn Rogerson. She and her whole family will always be closer than kin, the Hawthornes to my Kellys.

The hugest of huge thanks are owed to Elizabeth Harding, my incomparable agent, who was there for every panicked email and who talked me through each big decision with the utmost patience. Sarah Gerton, assistant agent at Curtis Brown, provided excellent feedback that challenged me to dig deeper on each of my books. My editor, Alexandra Cooper, saw what this story could become and helped it into its fullest form. Without Alyssa Miele, Bethany Reis, and Valerie Shea, *Where the Watermelons Grow* would have been filled with 100 percent more typos and awkward phrases (and Miss Lorena would've been driving an amazing shape-shifting car-van!). And Erin Fitzsimmons created the cover and jacket design of my heart.

Last but most definitely not least, I am beyond grateful for my husband, Mahon, and my daughter, Kate (whose toddler antics heavily inspired Mylie). Y'all are my world.